FAILED VISION

ANDRÉE ROBY

*To Kay
an amazing
lady + artist.
Best wishes
Andrée Roby
x

Nov 2020*

© 2020 Andrée Roby

Cover Illustrations: Micaela Grove & Jaco Du Plooy

Editing: Régine Demuynck

Publisher: Régine Demuynck

ISBN: 9798679002241

All rights reserved.

PREFACE

I knew after publishing 'Double Vision' that I would write a prequel, 'Failed Vision'. It took me a while, as knowing that the end of the story cannot be changed, made it a different and challenging way to write.

I could not have written 'Failed Vision' without the input from two fabulous people, my daughter Micaela Grove and her boyfriend, Jaco Du Plooy. Our brainstorming sessions have kept me going. The cover is a joint effort too and I am truly grateful for their time and commitment to this story.

My sincere thanks to my friends Sue and Norma who have proof-read the book, and given me valuable feedback on the storyline.

Thanks to Joanna Warrington, a fellow author, for putting me on the right track by encouraging me to rewrite the beginning of the book, and for her expert help throughout.

I am grateful to the readers of 'Double Vision' who have been waiting for the prequel for months. They have kept me motivated to complete the story and I thank them for their loyalty and enthusiasm for my words.

AMANDA - 2018

PROLOGUE

As she walked away from the scene of the arrest of Vince O'Shaughnessy's murderer, Amanda thought she had done a good day's work. Although still shaken from the events that had unfolded that evening, she was exhilarated to know that another killer had been identified, arrested and hopefully would be behind bars for a long time.

She flopped on the back seat of the police car despatched to take her home, her body aching with weariness. The adrenaline that had pumped through her during her frightening confrontation with the murderer, was now leaving her exhausted and spent. It had been a pretty intense evening. Closing her eyes, she rested her head back to relax. Unfortunately, the now familiar and haunting thought of a more sinister event engulfed Amanda yet again. Deep sadness and intense guilt washed over Amanda at the oddest times. The frequency of which had not diminished since the dreadful summer of 2017.

God, if only there was a way to stop thinking back to that summer and stop the guilt in my heart. So many "If onlys."

Amanda had worked hard to come to terms with what she saw as her failed vision. She had helped the police find many missing persons, but the one time which mattered the most to her, she had failed.

Why did it happen in the first place?

She had asked herself this question a thousand times, in a thousand different ways. No answer ever erased the horror of that summer. The nightmare lived on…

AMANDA - 2016

[1]

"Nathan! I am talking to you. Can you please pick up Kelly from school this afternoon? And check with the teachers if she was okay during the day. She had tummy pains again last night. I was going to pick her up, but I've been called by a police station in London, near Southwark. They asked me to come in and talk to them about me helping more local police stations with missing person cases. I'm unlikely to be back on time to pick her up. Can you do it? Nathan?"

It was hard at the best of times to get Nathan's attention, but when he was involved in work on his computer it was worse. Amanda was losing patience with him. His constant working had been the bane of their life since living together. It had caused a rift in their relationship and affected their daughter Kelly. The eight-year old often wondered where her daddy was and why he was always working. What was she supposed to tell her that she had not already said?

Amanda was juggling her work as a waitress in a restaurant and the readings for her regulars, and new clients. Occasionally she worked on a police case for a missing person or a missing body. She had finally taken the plunge and made herself available to her local nick. That was a year ago and she had no regret. She loved her work as a psychic detective and she had already solved two cases.

Her first case had been to find a missing man in his twenties, suffering from mental health issues. The family was concerned about him committing suicide if left alone too long. With her help, he was found in a disused warehouse near Tulse Hill: he had been living in squalor for two days, without food or water. Sadly, he had a jerry can full of petrol and a box of matches. He was planning to set the warehouse on fire with him inside. The extreme relief at finding him was a feeling Amanda had never experienced before.

Her second case involved a paedophile in the East End who had groomed a child on the internet then arranged to meet him. He then raped and strangled him. However, he had bragged online about killing the boy. When arrested, he refused to tell the police where he had disposed of the body.

Her success with her first case had been

mentioned to several inspectors in the South London area. That had then led to the second request for help. That case had been much more laborious. After several attempts, she had a vision that the child's body was under a block of flats by the Thames, near the Tower of London. She had guided the detective and the police officers to a posh apartment block with a small quay jutting onto the Thames. Sure enough, the body was found under the jetty, buried in the seaweed and sediment left by the Thames at low tide. Although it was upsetting to witness the state of the body after several days spent in the water, Amanda was secure in the knowledge that the family had closure with a body to bury and mourn. She felt tremendous sorrow for the mother of that child. It was impossible to even imagine her reaction should Kelly be groomed, abducted and then killed by a paedophile. It did not bear thinking about.

Right now, she needed to know that Nathan would pick up their daughter from school and that all would be well. She would be safe. The downside of her job with the police was that it made Amanda worry more about her child's safety. Especially after she caught glimpses of gruesome pictures in several incident rooms. They had churned her stomach.

"Yes, I will!" came the exasperated, belated response from Nathan. "But I need to go to a job in

Camberwell around eight o'clock tonight, so you have to be back on time."

"I'll do my best. I'll text you if I have a problem. Thanks. See you later."

Amanda was driving to Southwark in South London which should take her about fifty minutes. It was lunchtime and the traffic was unpredictable. She came to a standstill after fifteen minutes. While sitting there she found herself thinking back with nostalgia to Kelly's first day at school. It had been a momentous event, her little girl, starting primary school. Her mind drifted to that happy morning.

"Mummy, look at me. Daddy, you like my uniform?" Kelly had twirled with a beaming smile.

Kelly had been super excited to wear her school uniform for her first day at school. Having turned five a few months before, she was joining the Year One class at her local primary school.

"Daddy, take a photo please." She had stretched the last word and looked at him cutely to ensure her dad complied with her request.

"Okay, just a minute Kelly. Alright, smile. Lovely. I've taken a few and we can WhatsApp them to Grandma Reine, Uncle Joe, Uncle Tony and Uncle Josh. Let's go."

She had sauntered happily between her parents and got into Amanda's car, sitting gingerly in the child seat, waiting for Nathan to buckle her up. She had visited the school recently and liked it. While Amanda had been plaiting her long brown hair, Kelly had confided that she loved learning. Today she was particularly happy to have both parents take her to school. She had told Amanda that, in her opinion, Daddy was away an awful lot. She did not understand why he needed to be absent that much. She wanted to spend time with him, but he was always busy.

"Grown-ups are weird, Mummy. They are always busy. I think Daddy never has fun…"

Hum! Wise observations for such a young child. Her mother reflected.

Amanda had been both proud of Kelly's wisdom and sad for her child who was missing out on valuable time with her father. She always found it hard to understand that Kelly was not as much of a priority to Nathan as she was for her. At least Kelly's first day at school had been a happy day for everyone.

Bored with the radio, Amanda put a cd on. Elvis's melodious music made her heart leap with joy as it always did. Her favourite song was on. Amanda knew Elvis had not written it as a tribute to his wife, Priscilla, as she had first thought. The song talked about his love of God. But to Amanda the title itself took on a whole new dimension when Kelly was born. "The wonder of you" was how she viewed Kelly from the moment she was born.

She remembered vividly how her heart had melted at the sight of her baby daughter when she was born. She had been in awe of her pink fingers all curled up in little fists, at the brown fluff on her head, at her cute round face. Above all, she was fascinated by her eyes which had already opened and looked up at her, her mummy. Amanda had never experienced such a strong love welling up inside of her. Kelly had been a true wonder for Amanda. It was sad that this happy memory brought up a bitter-sweet memory too. That of glancing at the other beds around her in the maternity ward and envying the joy on the faces of parents welcoming their new baby together. Alone since she had gone into labour the night before, she had not been able to stop the sadness that had tainted what should have been a perfect day.

On Kelly's first journey to school, mother and daughter had sung the Elvis' song. Having listened to it so often in the car, Kelly loved it too. Especially as she knew the song reminded Amanda of Kelly. The child thought it super cool to be called a wonder.

"Come on you, moron, move along. We haven't got all day." Beep! Beep!

Amanda heard the driver shout out of his car

window behind her. In her dream state, she had failed to notice that the traffic was moving and she was holding people up. She waved her hand in apology to the angry face she saw in the rear-view mirror and moved on. She wondered if Nathan would remember to pick up Kelly or if she ought to remind him nearer the time. She decided to let him be for the rest of the day. Meanwhile she had to negotiate the busy roads of London and this was a challenge she never enjoyed.

At home, Nathan was working hard. He had made a few phone calls and was waiting for his brother/boss, Josh, to give him the instructions about a job this evening. He set an alarm to remind him to pick up Kelly.

His mind wandered to Amanda.

If she knew I take Kelly with me on jobs instead of being at home, she would have a fit. Kids are amazing though. I can't believe Kelly is keeping quiet about this. I never asked her not to say anything and yet she knows it's best not to tell her mother. Smart girl. Mind you, she did whinge not long ago about finding it scary when I take too long. Give her credit though, it can't be fun waiting for me alone in the car. The problem is that most of the times I am back quickly but often it takes ages. Frankly I don't see how things can be different. I need to earn money and Amanda too. It's not as if we even have relatives nearby to take care of Kelly. Reine and the uncles are far away and my parents are both dead. What exactly am I expected to do?

This had been an on-going dilemma for Nathan. Who was there to leave Kelly with? He had to take her with him even though she did not like it. There was no choice. Work was work and it paid the bills. Nathan was a champion at convincing himself that his actions were wholly justified. In his opinion, Amanda was nagging him all the time now and it was getting on his nerves. He wanted to be with her and Kelly, it's just that it was not that pleasant a relationship at times.

I guess I can't blame her entirely. I know I wasn't at the hospital with Amanda when she was in labour. I've lived with the guilt of missing Kelly's birth for eight years now. And she won't let me forget about it. As if I'd done it on purpose. I had to attend to urgent business and that had to come first. Get over it.

To distract himself from wondering how old Kelly would have to be before he was let off the hook, Nathan made his way to the kitchen. As he was getting himself a snack, his mobile rang:

"Hello? Hi Josh. What's up?"

"You know that job I told you about for tonight, you need to go earlier. The punters have heard you're coming. It's unlikely you'll be able to collect the money as the buggers will hide or refuse to answer the door. You need to surprise them when they come back from picking their kids up from school. They won't expect you then. Go there around three o'clock."

"Hang on Josh, I can't. I have to pick up my kid from school at three today and take her home because Amanda is at work. Can't I go a bit later?"

"Nathan, I've just told you. You need to surprise them. Why don't you take your kid with you as soon as you pick her up and go collect my money? It's not as if you've never taken her to work before. What's the problem now?"

"Usually I take her with me when I know Amanda will be late, but today she might be back soon after Kelly finishes school. How am I gonna explain that to her, eh?"

"Listen Nat, that's your problem, bro. I have a job that needs doing and I'm telling you when it needs doing. Take it or leave it. I can find another guy. But your cut is two hundred and fifty big ones, you might want to think twice about not going. I expect you to show up later in my office with the money you've collected."

Josh Stark was not the compromising type. He was a flashy, luxury-loving, selfish guy who had never married, let alone had kids. He only had himself to take into account hence his total lack of understanding of the restrictions a married man with a kid had. Nathan was in a quandary. Was it feasible for him to pick up Kelly then zoom over to Camberwell? From what he had been told, the wife was at work and the husband was supposed to be off sick. But he had been reported doing odd jobs for cash in hand. They pleaded poverty when the time came to pay the rent, but Josh had got a mate of his to take pictures of the husband at work. He had WhatsApped them to Nathan. His instructions were to use them to lean on the alleged sick father if he was reluctant to cough up the rent money. Nathan did not relish these confrontations. He preferred cool, calm and collected punters. They were few and far between.

At three o'clock, he was at Kelly's school gates. As soon as they opened, he darted inside, pushing ahead of the waiting mothers. He had no time to worry if they thought him rude. Right now he did not care if his image of a well-mannered dad was in jeopardy. Nathan was on a mission to fetch Kelly, and right now disgruntled mothers were lost on his radar. He entered the classroom, took Kelly by the hand, collected her coat and made his way to the car with her. Asking the teacher about how Kelly had been that day was far from his mind, as was remembering to take her lunchbox with them. Camberwell beckoned and that was his focus. He was practically dragging Kelly behind him and got to the car in record time.

"Daddy, why are we rushing? I don't want to run. My tummy is still a bit sore. Slow down, Daddy."

"Stop whingeing. We have to go and do an urgent job for Uncle Josh. Now be a good girl and get in the car. I am in a hurry."

Kelly got in the car in silence. Even at eight years old, she knew better than to argue. She loved her daddy dearly, but it scared her when Nathan was impatient with her or when he dragged her to different places for his work. She knew Mummy was not aware that she was often with Nathan in his car instead of being at home. Mummy would not be happy about this, and Kelly did not tell her. But she did not like it when she was left in the car waiting for Nathan to return from visiting one of Uncle Josh's clients. She had even been brave enough to tell her daddy about it once. He had not been pleased with her. She had decided to keep quiet about this too! She had noticed that Mummy had been crying quite a bit recently and that, when Nathan was home, often they were annoyed at each other and argued. Kelly wanted to hide under her duvet when she heard them. She was frightened. She wanted her mummy to be fine because she loved her very much. It upset her when her mum cried and she did not like her dad much on those days.

But now she was in the car with him and she was starving. The teacher had said it was alright for her not to eat lunch if her tummy was still sore. She hadn't eaten anything, and now that she was better, she was hungry.

"Do you have a snack for me, Daddy? I had no lunch today coz my tummy hurt. You left my lunchbox at school and I'm starving."

"Christ, what now? Why didn't you tell me about your lunchbox? No, I don't have a snack. If I can, I will stop and grab some food."

He was in such a bad mood that she forced herself to be still and not say a word until they got home, in case he made her cry like he did her mummy. She just wanted to go home, to play with her fluffy teddy bear and her doll instead of being here, but she had no choice. She decided to grin and bear it and not complain even though she was starving...

[2]

"Mummy, Mummy, I want my Mummy."

The wails from the child were louder with each word. Passers-by were ignoring the little girl in school uniform, crying and asking for her mummy. It is not that they were uncaring, it was more because, in that part of London, people had learned to mind their own business. They knew not to take anything they saw at face value. This supposedly lost child may be a decoy for a mugger or worse, a murderer. Although a few people wondered about her, their self-preservation instinct won. They walked on, head down, to avoid looking at her.

This was why Kelly had been wandering the streets of Camberwell for ten minutes, alone, upset, crying yet unchallenged. She was deeply ashamed too because she had been so frightened earlier on that she had peed in her knickers. Her school socks and shoes were all wet. Daddy will be cross for sure. If only she remembered where he was and how to get back to the car. She had been crying for a long time now and had lost track of the time. Surely Daddy must be worried by now. How will he find her in this big place full of grown-ups who went past and said nothing to her? She was scared, feeling abandoned and guilty for having left her daddy's car earlier on. What about Mummy? Oh no. Daddy will have to tell her she was on a job with him and Mummy will know. The thought of not having told the full truth to her mother made Kelly cry even more.

She thought back to what had happened to lead her here. It had taken a while to get to where Daddy needed to be in Camberwell (wherever that was). He had refused to stop to buy her a snack as he had promised. She thought this place was far from her school and from home. She was silently cross with him and her tummy kept rumbling, making awful noises, giving her pains as if her stomach was eating itself. It was a horrible pain. Worse than the tummy pains she had felt the night before. She wished she had not listened to the teacher who told her to leave her lunch and to just have water. She did not know this new pain and she thought it was hunger but maybe she had suddenly got a terrible disease. She just did not know, she was too young to know anyway.

From the back seat, she looked at her dad who was driving way too fast. Her upset was increasing as her hunger was getting worse.

That is unfair. He said he would stop and now he isn't. I don't like Daddy right now. I want to be at home with Mummy. At least she would give me a fruit or some biscuits. Daddy is horrible today. Maybe when he stops and leaves me in the car, I can go out and get a snack by myself. I am a big girl. I've been to the shops with Mummy. I know what to do, and Daddy keeps a few coins in the car. That's what I'll do but I won't tell him, like that he won't tell me off or anything.

Having found a solution to deal with her hunger, Kelly felt chuffed that she had made such a grown-up decision. Proud of her plan, she listened to Nathan telling her to stay in the car, assuring her he would only be ten minutes, fifteen max, and instructing her to keep the doors locked. She had nodded at him, armed with the knowledge that she might soon be eating a snack. Then she would come back to the car without him realising what she had done. She felt extremely brave.

As soon as Nathan had gone through the dirty, graffiti-covered door of the blocks of flats he was visiting, Kelly cautiously opened the door of the car.

She had unbuckled her belt. She had watched her parents do that often, and she too knew what to do. She noticed a group of kids, a bit older playing with a football under the laundry lines on the side of the building. By the entrance, where Nathan had gone in, she suddenly saw a group of teenagers, quite rowdy, pulling cigarettes from their pockets, ready to light them. One of them spotted her in the distance and elbowed one of his mates.

"Look over there bro, what's this kid doing here? That's a posh uniform, not from around here for sure. Come. Let's go talk to her. Maybe she has some money for us."

They approached nonchalantly and Kelly suddenly felt frightened, unsure if the two big boys coming towards her were friendly or not. She thought of going back to the car which was near, but her tummy rumbled loudly and she knew she needed to eat soon. She saw them get nearer, puffing on their cigarettes, looking arrogant and rather threatening. She was rooted to the spot. What did they want? What should she do? All of a sudden, she lost control and felt a humiliating trickle of wee running down her legs. She burst out crying, lost, humiliated, frightened, and now the object of the boys' laughter. They circled her. Both were looking her up and down, laughing at her.

"What have we here? A little cry baby with wet knickers? Oh dear, posh gal. What are your folks gonna say? Have you got money? Let's have a look in your pocket, come here. Don't be scared!"

The gobbier of the two was pulling at the pocket of her school blazer and found the few coins she had picked up in Nathan's car.

"A piddling four quid, won't go far with that. You have more? Come on, give it here."

The two boys were scaring her so she made a run for it. The fear propelled her forward, making her push past them and running in the opposite direction from the flats. Their laughter rang loud in her ears but luckily they did not pursue her. She was not worth the effort in their eyes. They had enjoyed scaring her and taking the piss but running after her required too much energy. Besides, they had plans with their mates.

She carried on running up the street. She thought it was the one they had come down by car, where she had seen some shops. Unknown to the boys, she had kept a two-pound coin held tightly in her right fist. They had not noticed it when they had robbed her. She guessed she should have gone back to the car but her stomach was making her common sense evaporate. She was just driven by the need to find anything that would take the hunger pain away.

She reached the top of the road without having seen a single shop. There were only houses. No shops. She was disappointed but would not give up. She decided to turn left but the more she walked the more houses she saw. Still no shop. How far should she go to find one? She kept going and came to a junction of two major roads. She thought she could see a shop up a road opposite. She carefully crossed the road and made her way up the street on her right. About halfway she saw the shop front she had seen in the distance. It was not a shop she could buy food in. She felt gutted.

She carried on until, finally, she saw a newsagent. She sighed with relief and walked in, holding the coin in her fist as if her life depended on it. She picked up a bag of crisps, a juice and a bar of chocolate. She was trying to add up the price like her mummy had taught her. She was so shaky and hungry that she did not manage to count on her fingers. She brought her treasure to the till and gave her two-pound coin.

"That's not enough, you need fifty pence more."

The shop keeper was looking at her with stern eyes and she got frightened again. She did not have enough to buy all the items. Hesitating for a bit, she chose to keep the chocolate bar and the carton of juice. She pushed the crisps aside.

"Harry, don't be mean to the poor child. Can't you see she's upset? She must be hungry. Come on, take the crisps as well, I'll give you the fifty pence."

These magical words came out from behind her. She turned around to face a badly dressed man, his face all wrinkled, his body stooped forward, leaning on a walking stick. He looked quite old to her.

Kelly had been warned many times by Amanda not to accept money or sweets or anything, from a stranger. Right now though, the offer of fifty pence to secure the three items was too tempting to resist. She said thanks to the kind stranger, took her goods and left the shop in such a hurry that she went the wrong way. By the time she realised what she had done, she did not know how to get back to where Nathan had left the car. She started to panic and cry for her mother.

Two blocks away, Nathan had reached his car and, on opening the door, realised that it was empty. He was scared and angry too.

What the hell? Oh shit where is Kelly? Kelly, Kelly, stop being silly, come here Kelly. Where are you? It is no time to play hide and seek you stupid girl, Kelly, come on. Kelly.

In his panic Nathan kept calling her over and over. He saw the group of boys looking at him as he was looking inside, around, and underneath his car like a mad man. One boy, taking pity on him, came up to him and asked if he was looking for the little girl in the school uniform.

"Yes, I am, have you seen her? Please, where is she?"

"Don't know where she is now man, but she was here, crying. Two boys were around her and took her money. She ran away from them, in that direction but I ain't seen her since. I guess it was about fifteen minutes ago."

"Thank you, thank you. What a relief. She did not go with anyone did she? Please tell me, did you see her go with anybody?"

"No man, I told you she just ran off up the street. Not sure what she was looking for but that's the direction she went. Sorry got to go in now, or my mum will scalp me. Good luck man."

He joined his mates and they all went into the building to their respective families, leaving Nathan frantically searching for Kelly. It was five o'clock and in late September it started getting dark early. He was not sure where to look or where to start.

He breathed deeply and reviewed his options.

1. *I could take the car and drive around to see if I could spot her.*

2. *I could wait a while longer and see if she came back to the car or*
3. *I could call the cops and report her missing straight way in case she met with an unsavoury character and got hurt or kidnapped.*

He was panicking now thinking of Amanda.

Oh shit, I have to tell Amanda. What am I gonna tell her? I can't phone her now, she will be worried sick and furious and it won't help find Kelly. But she works with the cops, they might help Amanda by putting more men on the beat to look for Kelly. What to do? Shit, shit, shit! I just don't know.

His mobile was ringing. Without looking at the screen he answered: "Kelly? Is that you? Where are you?"

"Nathan? What's going on? It's me Amanda, why did you ask if it was Kelly? Is she not at home with you? What's happened? Nathan what is going on for God's sake?"

"Amanda, she's gone, she was in the car but now she's gone. She was supposed to wait for me in the car but she ran away and I don't know where she is. I'm sorry Amanda."

"Hang on a minute, where are you? You are supposed to be at home and I am on my way back so you can go to your job. Why did Kelly leave the car without you, I don't understand."

"I guess I better tell you the truth. We're in Camberwell. Josh insisted that I come to do the job planned for tonight in the afternoon as the punters would be home. I had to be here just after three o'clock, so I had to drive straight from school. There was no time to go home. I had to take Kelly with me. She said she was hungry but I didn't stop to buy a snack. Maybe she went to get one. Shall I ring the cops? I'm sorry Amanda, I only left her in the car ten minutes. Promise."

"Oh my God Nathan, my baby! Why on earth did you take her on a job with you? Where is she? What if she is hurt? She must be frightened. You moron." Amanda was getting more and more hysterical.

"I swear, she better be found unharmed or your life won't be worth living. You are a fucking irresponsible idiot. You and your bloody work. I have had it. I'm not too far from Camberwell, tell me where you are. I'll make my way there. And call the cops right now!"

It was unusual for her to swear but, these days, Nathan had the knack of bringing out the worst in her more and more frequently.

Nathan told her where he was and then kept

quiet, fearing he might increase Amanda's anger towards him. Not normally a believer, he nevertheless made a quick appeal towards the sky for Kelly to be safe, wondering if he should have gone looking for her after all. He was pacing around his car while dialling 999 when he saw a child walking towards him. She was holding the hand of a matronly woman, whose face showed obvious concern and sympathy. He aborted the call and ran at full speed, gathering Kelly up in his arms, crying out of sheer relief.

"Kel, where did you go? God, Kelly I have been worried sick. Where were you? Why did you leave the car? Someone might have hurt you?" He was hugging her so hard she wriggled in his arms to shrug him off her and loosen his hold. As he put her down, she looked sheepish and contrite.

"Daddy! I'm sorry. I was hungry and you didn't stop to buy food and I took coins and I got out of the car and the boys took my money but I had one coin in my hand and I am sorry, Daddy, I peed in my pants and I ran off and I walked and walked and found a shop and I got lost and I wanted Mummy and then this lady stopped and helped me find this building and the car."

Her words were tumbling out of her, propelled by sheer relief at finding her dad again, at being safe although feeling guilty for leaving the car. At last, she stopped to take a breath.

"I am sorry, Daddy, I won't do it again I promise."

"Oh Kelly, I'm happy you're back. What a relief. Thank you for bringing her back here. I am very grateful to you, thank you."

He had turned to face the woman who had taken the trouble to bring Kelly back and he felt like giving her a hug too.

"It's okay. Glad we found you. Poor little thing, crying for her mama outside my house. I wasn't gonna leave her alone, poor kid. When she described where the car was and the building you went in, I knew where you was. Here she is."

She was smiling at Nathan, whilst wondering what kind of a father would lose track of where his kid was. Even she knew where her four brats were at any time.

On impulse, Nathan hugged the woman, like a man drowning holds on to a lifebuoy. He was immensely grateful to this kind person who had brought his daughter back, unharmed. She meant a lot to him. He could never imagine Kelly not being in his life.

A flashback to the first time he had laid eyes on Kelly came to his mind. Although he had missed her birth, he had showed up at the hospital a few hours after she was born. He had bought a teddy bear for his daughter and a big bunch of flowers for Amanda. He had seen Amanda in the distance with the baby in her arms and his heart had leapt. What a beautiful sight they both made. He had caught a glimpse of other couples, sitting together, holding their babies. He had approached slowly, thinking how beautiful Amanda looked and feeling excited at seeing the little bundle held against her mother's breast.

He had heard Amanda whisper to the baby: "Baby, this is your wayward daddy. Nathan, meet your daughter, Kelly. I hope you don't mind but I decided on her name. I know we had chosen a few, but when I saw her this morning, she reminded me of my beloved grandmother. It was her name and it suits her. What do you think?"

"I like it, Kelly is a nice name. Wow, she is gorgeous, can I hold her please? Hello baby, I'm your daddy. I am sorry I was not there to welcome your arrival. I promise I won't miss anything again."

"Oh, she has my eyes don't you think? But she has your face, she'll be pretty. Thank you, Amanda, our baby is perfect, I'm so happy."

Nathan had never experienced love as pure as the one flooding his heart at that moment. His love for his baby daughter had been mixed with optimism for the future, with a strong sense of wanting to protect her, with an even stronger sense of duty and a need to provide everything for his only child. He clearly recalled his silent promise to Kelly.

You will want for nothing, beautiful child of mine. I will do my job well. Whatever the future holds for you and whatever you become, I will protect you. I will be by your side as your life unfolds.

As he had done that day, he promised himself again that he would do whatever was needed to protect Kelly. Always.

[3]

Despite her relief to hear that Kelly was back safely with Nathan, whilst driving home to join them, Amanda's anger was taking on huge proportions and it was hard to focus on her driving. She couldn't believe that he had acted so irresponsibly. The child had come back unharmed. But what would have happened if she had been kidnapped or had got lost? She didn't want to imagine this scenario. She knew too much about what some children had endured in the hands of evil people.

She was furious with Nathan. Their relationship had not been that great of late and this latest incident did not encourage her to be lenient or forgiving. She had always known he was work-focussed. After all, this was the reason they had broken up in the first place when they were young adults. But after Kelly's birth, her hope had been that he would spend more time with the two of them.

Officially Nathan worked four days a week with Josh who had a debt recovery business in South East London. He employed Nathan to collect the arrears from his clients. Amanda sighed at the unwelcome thought of the man with whom she never got on. She was sensitive to people's energy and, whenever in Josh's presence, a queasiness came over her. For this reason, she chose to remain distant from him. She had mentioned her uneasiness to Nathan, who hadn't understood her reluctance to mix with his brother. This issue had caused many arguments between them in the past. Her intuition, when she had first met him, had told her that Josh was bad news.

The traffic had hit rush hour and it would take her at least half an hour to get home. She was eager to hold Kelly but, in all honesty, she would prefer not to see Nathan. She was resentful and angry towards him. She suddenly wondered what her life would be like right now if she had never laid eyes on this man.

She had met Nathan Stark when they were both at a sixth form college. She had found him attractive from the moment she'd entered one of the classrooms at the beginning of year twelve. He had been sitting alone, in the back row, away from his peers, head down, slyly using his phone under the desk. He had brown hair then, slightly too long to meet school regulations. In her opinion, it needed a good combing and trimming but she'd thought his hairstyle gave him an air of being laid back. She'd liked that. When he heard someone come in, he had looked up towards the door. He'd nodded his head slightly in her direction then unfurled his slim built body from his chair to greet her. She had estimated that he was probably around five foot eleven. His face was attractive, with high cheekbones, full lips and slightly slanted brown eyes.

Nathan had stared at her and then smiled in Amanda's direction. She had been taken aback by how he greeted her.

"Hi there pretty girl, I am Nathan. What's your name? Come and sit near me."

Before Amanda had been able to answer him, he had grabbed her arm, pulling her towards the seat next to his.

"Wait! I'm Amanda, and I prefer to sit nearer the front. Maybe I'll meet you after class, alright?"

He had shrugged and nodded. She'd guessed he was unhappy to have to wait. She had felt his appraising stare pierce into her back as she had taken a seat in the front row. She had forced herself not to turn to look at him or react to him.

For the next two academic years, Nathan and Amanda had spent time together whenever they had free study periods and in the evenings. Most weekends Nathan had been busy with various projects. They would go out dancing occasionally on a Saturday evening or go to the cinema, but their relationship was nothing like the ones her friends had with their boyfriends. This disparity had made Amanda question her love for Nathan on many occasions.

After their exams the following year, Amanda and Nathan lost sight of each other. Their relationship had fizzled out. He had been busier than ever. She had drifted away from him. She had come to the conclusion that there was no future with Nathan. At least not the sort of future she had known she deserved. Thinking back to that time, she ought to have stuck to that knowledge and never got near Nathan Stark again.

She was still questioning her love for Nathan as she opened the front door. On hearing her mother coming home, Kelly rushed into her arms, breathless and in tears. She whispered in her mother's ear:

" Mummy, I was very scared. I thought I was lost. I peed myself coz I was scared. And Mummy, I am sorry I didn't tell you about Daddy taking me to his work. I love you to the moon and back. I thought you would be upset if I told you. I am sorry, Mummy. I won't wander off and I won't lie to you ever again, I promise, Mummy."

Amanda's tears were mingling with Kelly's as the child sobbed and sobbed. She hugged Kelly more tightly, her heart aching for her daughter.

"There, darling. It's alright, you're safe now. Mummy is here. I'll protect you and never let you go. Hush now. "

It had been a huge shock to learn that afternoon, that Kelly had been with Nathan at work not only today but also on previous occasions. When Amanda had thought her at home, she had actually been alone in his car instead. She knew full well that the areas in which Josh had properties were dangerous. Definitely not the right places to leave a young child who is not street-savvy, alone in a car. What upset her more than anything was that both daughter and father had shared a secret.

I guess I've to thank my lucky star that it all came out now. I can't believe he took her on jobs before and they've not said anything about it. What am I supposed to do and think? How can I trust Nathan again? Why didn't Kelly tell me? What if she had been hurt? How would I ever forgive him if harm had come to her?

She had to stop dwelling on what she saw as a betrayal and confront Nathan with the events of the afternoon. She noticed he had not come to the door to greet her. He was probably in his office. A discussion was necessary about today's incident and his irresponsibility. She took Kelly to her bedroom and stayed with her until the child was calmly playing with her dolls. She then went to find Nathan.

Amanda knocked on the door of the office and went in. Nathan was on his mobile. Looking sheepish, he turned around to acknowledge her. He mouthed the word Police to her. Intrigued, and apprehensive, she stood and listened to the one-sided conversation.

"I understand, officer, but I was only away for ten minutes. I had to deliver a letter urgently to a client and she was told to stay in the car."

"...."

"Yes I do realise that I shouldn't have left a child her age alone. The problem is I had to go up several floors and the building has no lift. Because Kelly had not been feeling well the day before, I decided to leave her in the car. I had no idea she would wander off and get lost."

"...."

"A lady brought her back to the car. Kelly had been crying outside her house. Yes, I did ask for her name. She wrote it on a piece for paper for me. Hold on, I'll check it now. She was called Jalissa Akumbe. I don't know her address, sorry."

"…."

"Why? I don't understand. Why do you have to call social services? It's not as if anything has happened. And that sort of incident has never happened before. Then why do you have to inform social services? This seems unnecessary to me."

"…."

"Of course my daughter was not in danger! And she is well cared for. For god sake, my wife works for various police stations in South London. Do you think we would neglect our daughter? This is ludicrous."

Amanda's anger which had abetted when she'd arrived home and held Kelly, was now rising again. Why was Nathan talking about social services? Why were the police calling Nathan and what was going on exactly? She waved to Nathan and mouthed to him "what the hell is going on?"

Nathan signalled to her to be quiet and wait. He listened to the person on the other end of the line a while longer and then said goodbye. He put the phone down slowly and took a few seconds before addressing Amanda.

"That was the police. They rang my number back because I had dialled 999 and interrupted the call.

They were checking I was alright, and they asked the reason why I had dialled emergency services. They are cracking down on jokers who ring for nothing. I had to tell them that I was going to report my daughter missing but that she had just returned. I told them the truth, but it seems they now think social services should be involved.

"Are you a total moron or what? Did it not occur to you that they may be unhappy and unimpressed about what you did today? Just as I am!"

Amanda was not only furious but was now worried about a potential visit from social services with all the impact it could have on their future as parents and on Kelly.

"Today is going from bad to worse. As if you taking Kelly to your work, and her going missing, wasn't bad enough, now the police and social services are involved. What possessed you Nathan?

"Shut up Amanda. I've messed up, yes, but I have to work. How do you think the bills get paid in this household? You are always reproaching me that I'm working but we need the money I earn. I had to do a job for Josh and there was not time to take Kelly home. Oh, but hang on. That wouldn't have been any good either as I can't leave her alone. She is too young for that too. What was I supposed to do

Amanda? Come on, tell me as you seem to know everything."

Nathan was upset and not proud of himself. Going on the defensive was easier than trying to pacify Amanda and apologise.

"I'm lost for words Nathan. I'm struggling with your irresponsibility, your absence and just about everything in this relationship right now. I think we need to think where we are going. I'm unhappy Nathan. I can't go to work and feel at peace if I know that you are not taking care of Kelly seriously. I look after her myself as much as possible but, at times I need you to step in. Your job is more flexible than mine and it's not often that you have to take care of Kelly. "

It was taking all her self-control not to throw Nathan out of the flat that night. He had admitted it was a mistake but, given what she had learnt, she found it hard to accept his explanation. That had been a repeated event not just a one off. He happened to have got caught out this time.

I can't believe I thought us being together would be a good thing. What a fool I have been. Indirectly I too put Kelly's life in danger. He has always been irresponsible and nothing has changed from when we were teenagers. But that's it now. No more chances.

She had come to the end of her tether and she had just made a decision.

That's it. It's over. I can't take any more.

As she repeated the words in her mind, she felt her resolve grow stronger. She had to end this relationship for her sake and Kelly's, concentrate on her work and raise her daughter on her own. Kelly would see her father but, if social services were going to be involved, Nathan's visits with his daughter may be under supervision. It all depended on what the police told social services.

What a mess. I can see why Social Services might not trust him with his child. I don't trust him myself.

"I am tired, Nathan. We'll talk about this in a few days. We need to calm down and see what repercussions will come of this incident. I'll sleep with Kelly tonight. Goodnight."

"I'll be at work early tomorrow. Goodnight."

[4]

The following morning, Amanda had spoken to her mother about her decision. As expected Reine had played devil's advocate. She had put herself in Amanda's and Nathan's shoes to find a middle ground to benefit the couple and move their relationship forward in a more harmonious way.

Bless my mother, always the pacifier, doing her best to be fair. I know she wants to save us from splitting up, but my decision is final.

She aspired to be the type of mother to Kelly that Reine had been for her. They had had their disagreements when she was younger. What mother and daughter didn't? For Amanda, what mattered was that, in the end, they had become closer.

Amanda had been born with a gift of mediumship, but she had not been aware of it until her mother had brought it up. Reine had shown patience when explaining to Amanda why she kept seeing people at odd times of day or even night, people that others did not see. Before her fifteenth birthday, Amanda had rejected her gift which led her to become an unsettled, ill-at-ease teenager. Reine had showed her the importance of being true to herself and how disowning her gift was likely to make her life miserable. She encouraged her to attend mediumship circles and that had been her salvation. Amanda often acknowledged to herself that her mother had given birth to her twice. The day she was born and the day she got her to finally accept her gift.

During their conversation, Amanda had raised the issue of childcare and the challenges she would face by becoming a single, working mother. Reine had assured her that she was happy for Kelly to stay with her in the Lake District during the summer holiday. As Kelly was fond of her grandmother, that was a welcome solution. Her mother had offered to come down for all the shorter school holidays over the academic year. For emergencies likely to arise in her work with the police, she still had to find a reliable babysitter to look after Kelly at night and whenever necessary during the day.

It had been hard for Amanda to concentrate at

work the day after Kelly's disappearance. Her mind had been filled with the events of the previous day which had led her to make a life-changing decision. It had not been an easy one. She had spent the night going over what had happened in her life with Nathan and how they had got to that point.

After they had parted ways the summer they had sat their A Levels, she had never imagined that she would come across Nathan Stark again. It had seemed unlikely that she ever would. Within six months of splitting up with him, she had moved to South London from the Lake District where her mother and her brothers remained. She had found herself a small apartment and had worked part-time in a restaurant as a waitress. The owner had been happy to employ her on a part-time basis, mainly covering either the lunchtime or evening rush. It had been a small but nice restaurant in South Norwood and the clientele had been friendly. She had also been doing readings for money. She had grown more confident about her gift and had used it to better her life. She had enjoyed the emotional rewards which came from helping people by giving them guidance and comfort.

Amanda had been taken by surprise when, a few years later, she had recognised Nathan, sitting at a table in the restaurant one evening. He was meeting a potential business partner and he was pleased to see her. She had had mixed feelings about this encounter, although there was no denying that the physical attraction between them was still there. Nathan had been charming that night, and had arranged a date with her for the following week. She had wanted to go out casually for a while before rekindling a serious relationship. Like most women, she had been convinced that, this time around, he would change under her influence and that their relationship would be closer. They had enjoyed several outings together, a lot of passionate sex and thus grown close again. To her surprise, when he'd suggested they lived together in her flat, she had agreed.

A few months after Nathan had moved in, Amanda had discovered with a shock that she was pregnant. She had not planned to have a baby so soon after getting back together. She had been unsure of Nathan's reaction, thus she had shared the news with her mother first.

"Is there ever a right time, dear?" her mother had asked when Amanda told her of the pregnancy.

"You have been given a gift, take it, even if it means potentially being alone with the child in the future. I will help you, you know that."

Amanda had thought she was blessed to have the

mother that she did. Reine had always been supportive of her. She had plucked up the courage to tell Nathan about the pregnancy one evening they were having dinner together. Nathan had been shocked at first, then genuinely pleased. After a few days, the excitement at the prospect of becoming parents had become real. For the next few months after that, Amanda had believed in the miracle of being a close family soon, with Nathan spending time at home with her and the baby.

After eight years together, her hope had not quite materialised and right now she and Nathan had to talk further about the future of their relationship and what was best for their daughter. She had mentioned to him that they needed a few days to calm down and she had meant it. She didn't want to make the wrong decision. In her mind, Nathan also deserved a chance to reflect on the recent turn of events.

Two days later, Amanda asked Nathan if he would be home that night. She had come to the conclusion that the relationship was over and had planned to tell him he had one week to move his stuff out. She would then have to explain to Kelly why her father was no longer living at home. She was not looking forward to it. The child would be upset because, despite everything, she loved Nathan. But Amanda knew that Kelly was an observant child, and she had understood a lot with regards to her father's work.

That evening, Amanda thought that her discussion with Nathan might go better over a meal. She had picked up Kelly from school and they had spent an hour together, playing and reading. Amanda was now in the kitchen preparing the food before Nathan returned home. Kelly had finished playing in her room and had come down to the kitchen, pretending to get a glass of milk. She stood by the fridge, shifting from foot to foot, looking pensively at her mother. Amanda looked at her, waiting, sensing turmoil in her daughter's mind.

"Mummy? I think I know what job Daddy does now, but I don't know what you do. What's your real job then? Daddy says you speak to dead people and it's not normal. Are you not normal?"

It had been bothering Kelly not to understand what her mother did for a living. She knew she worked in a restaurant sometimes in the evening. She had been there with Daddy, and seen Mummy take people's orders and bring the dishes to the table. She had been proud of her mother's skills.

But she was struggling to understand why people often came to their flat. Mummy had explained that, when the people came to see her, they wanted her to read the cards and hear messages from people who were dead.

"Then why do they leave in tears, Mummy? Do they get sad messages?"

"They are happy tears, Kelly. Family members who have died want to tell their loved ones good things about the future or send loving messages. People who get these messages are not sad."

"Grown-ups are definitely weird. Why do they want to hear from dead people? They don't even talk anyway. I don't get it. How does it work anyway?"

"Well it's a good question, darling. When I was your age, even younger, I used to see shadowy figures and things like snippets of films of events that were going to happen. I didn't understand the reason I saw them, but I assumed everyone else did. One day I asked a friend if what she saw was similar to me. She laughed, said of course not and asked me about it. She never saw things the way I did. As I was a bit scared, I asked my mum. She explained to me why I was seeing things and told me she was a psychic medium too. Like me, Grandma Reine can see things happening and she can hear dead people talk to her. Put simply, I am a medium. I am like a body the spirits use to send messages to their loved ones."

All this talk was hard to grasp for Kelly. She was

aware of Amanda's other job, working with the police to find people who had been killed. She was proud that her mummy worked with the police.

"I know it sounds strange to you. I am lucky to be able to help people. I love what I do and now the best part of my job, Kelly, is working with the police. Remember, I explained to you that, not long ago, I had worked on a case to find a missing boy. If the police have trouble finding a person, then the detectives ask me if I can see where the victim or their body is. Thanks to my help, a family recently was able to bury their little boy who had gone missing. For weeks they had no idea where he was. This way I bring a bit of hope and relief at an upsetting time for families of victims. I am proud of my work. I choose to ignore people who don't understand it, or make fun of me, like your daddy often does."

Kelly understood finally what her mother did for a living. She had been a little curious to know how it all worked and how her mother found people. Amanda explained that, by holding an object from the missing person, she would normally get little snippets of information.

"Like mobile phones pick up signals from the tower and a radio picks up the signals from the radio wave, I pick up the signals from spirits. Then I see a series of pictures or short clips. Similar to those you watch on YouTube. "

It had made Kelly giggle to think her mummy was getting clips from dead people. How did she get them? Where did she watch them? Right now though, she had had enough of this conversation. She went back to her room to play with Dolly, her favourite doll. Amanda was left reflecting about tonight's discussion with Nathan. She had prepared the ingredients for dinner, ready to cook them when Nathan arrived. To take her mind off her problems, she went to watch the news for a few minutes.

On the local channel, she caught a glimpse of the picture of a young boy missing since the previous night. He had left his home in the night, unnoticed by his parents, and had not been seen since. It was almost twenty-four hours ago and the parents were obviously concerned. The newsreader reported that the police were appealing for information from anyone who might have seen the boy or knew of his whereabouts. He added that the boy was called Jamie Wilson, lived in Peckham and was only ten years old. He was wearing jeans, a light blue t-shirt, white trainers, a black puffer jacket. His parents were baffled as Jamie had taken with him his Spiderman backpack, and the video games he was fond of playing on his Xbox. The police thought it was a weird thing to do unless he had planned to meet another Xbox player. They were appealing to anyone who might be offered cheap video games in the area. Amanda felt an icy shudder run the length of her spine and thought this was just the beginning of a dark time for the boy and his family.

[5]

Nathan was exhausted after visiting a number of Josh's punters all day. Late afternoon, he had gone on to a meeting which had lasted longer than he had anticipated. Now he was rushing home, hopefully on time for dinner, as he had promised Amanda he would. He was not looking forward to dinner. He had a hunch their relationship was on borrowed time. As soon as he entered the flat, he saw that Amanda was in front of the TV, watching the news, looking as white as a sheet.

"Hi Amanda, what's wrong? You look as if you've seen a ghost. What happened? Oh! You know about the kid that's gone missing? It's all over the radio, I heard it in the car."

"Yes, I have just seen it. I have a bad premonition

about this disappearance, I sense this kid is in real trouble. I will get in touch with the police station tomorrow in case I can help. Anyway let's have dinner. Go get Kelly from her room please while I cook the steaks quickly. Then we'll talk after dinner. "

His stomach dropped. After the exchange they had had a few days ago, it was not a complete surprise to Nathan that something was afoot. The look on Amanda's face fuelled his apprehension.

Best get Kelly and have dinner. Then I'll find out what Amanda has in mind. I don't want to lose Kelly and all we've built together. That would be sad, crazy even. I hope we can work things out. It's obvious Amanda's made up her mind. Do I even get a say in whatever she decided? After all I am Kelly's parent too. She isn't going to take my kid from me that's for sure.

"Hey, how is my girl doing this evening? What are you playing with? Can I join you?"

"Daddy, Daddy, yippee, let's play with my dollies. I'll have Dolly and you have Ted. I'm the mummy and you'll be the dad."

"Okay, but Mummy is expecting us soon for dinner. Are you not hungry?"

"Yes, I am. Not as much as I was the other day when I got lost but I am hungry. Let's go help mummy. It will be fun."

Kelly's comment about that dreadful day gave him a jolt. He had regretted that day like nothing else in his life. It was impossible to change or erase what happened and the scars it might leave on all three of them. Kelly had been scared to go with him in the car yesterday to go to school. He hoped her reluctance would be short-lived. Amanda had been mad at him and furious about social services possibly being involved. In the end, they had received a call yesterday to inform them that no action would be taken. The social worker had suggested Nathan attends a parenting class, about which she would send him a leaflet. This outcome had been a relief for both parents. However his guilt was harder to shift.

To top it all, Josh had been furious at the mess Nathan had got himself into. His brother's anger was not out of concern for his younger sibling. Nothing like that. It was more because the cops might be sniffing near Josh's businesses and most of them were not entirely above board. Nathan was not pleased when his brother called him a fool. He certainly felt more and more like one these days. He had asked Josh to find him a place to live, if things went pear-shaped with Amanda. There were a few empty properties ready to move into, if or when, he got his marching orders from Amanda. It was not a prospect he relished, but he was in no position right now to argue against it. Better let things settle and work harder to raise money to get his own place.

With a faint smile on his face, Nathan thought that he might even be able to convince her to either stay together now or take him back in a little while. Amanda had told Nathan many times that arrogance was his middle name. He disagreed. He was just an optimist and a charmer when he wanted something badly enough to make the effort. After all, he had got her back after she had moved down to London, didn't he? The thought occurred to him, that if it had not been for her younger brother Tony telling him where to find her, he would not be playing with his precious daughter right this minute.

Yep, it was clever of me finding her in that restaurant in South Norwood. Good job I asked Tony where she had gone to. To be fair, I hadn't been too bothered about our relationship ending. I was young and immature then. I didn't realise how empty my heart would be after she left the area. It made me realise what a big mistake it was not to pay more attention to her, and to let her go. Still, it was brilliant to see her again when I organised our surprise meeting. I think this was the moment I knew for certain how much I'd missed her and how much I still loved her.

"Dinner is ready you two. Let's eat."

Shaking off the memories which now brought him more sadness than joy, he took Kelly in his arms like he used to do when she was little. She was giggling at her dad, telling him she was too old to be carried like a baby. Despite her protest, Kelly was happy being in her dad's arms. At the table, she sat between her parents, unaware of the impending change to her life. Nathan was on tenterhooks, hoping that the discussion with Amanda would turn out fine for the whole family. Amanda's mind was in conflict. It was unsettling to see Nathan interact with Kelly at diner. It magnified her guilt about breaking the family up. What had driven her decision was her absolute need to know that Kelly was safe when Amanda was at work. That Nathan was doing what he was supposed to when he was in charge of their daughter. But her trust in his ability to take care of her properly had been broken.

"Good girl, Kelly. Thanks for clearing up the dishes. Now please go to your room to play for a bit. I'll be up in a little while to read you a story. I need to talk to Daddy now."

Kelly did as she was told. She was in a hurry to tell Dolly the jokes her daddy had told her at dinner. She thought he had been funny. When Daddy was in that jolly mood he was lovely. When he was in a gloomy mood and all impatient, she didn't like him much. Briefly she wondered what Amanda had to say to him but soon forgot about it when she got to her bedroom.

Amanda was sitting opposite Nathan in the lounge. They looked at each other for a brief moment. Each knew what was at stake. Nathan was still hopeful that his hunch was wrong. To split up the family was a major step. He was squirming inside. He shifted in his seat when he saw Amanda look at him pensively as if about to speak. He was waiting to hear her.

"Nat, I am sorry but our relationship isn't working. We've got to the point of arguing constantly about your work, and frankly I don't trust you with Kelly any more. I'm unhappy and I can't live like that. Not being able to rely on you, Nathan, causes everyone too much stress. Both Kelly and I deserve better. I think it would be best if you moved out of the flat. Preferably within the week. We can discuss arrangements for Kelly once we know where you're going to live."

Although her mind was made up Amanda was struggling to stop her lip from trembling.

In the recess of his mind, Nathan acknowledged deep down that he had given the relationship his best shot. It was a shame he always fell short of her expectations. He understood where she was coming from and respected her for making a difficult decision. However, he was who he was, and he too, had come to the end of his tether.

"I'm sorry, truly sorry, it has come to that, you know. I am going to miss Kelly a lot. Not seeing her every day…. You know that I did spend time with her as often as my work allowed me to. But whatever effort I made, it seemed to go unnoticed. I am tired of not being good enough in your eyes. I'll ask Josh to find me somewhere to live and I hope Kelly is allowed to come and stay or at least visit me. I hope you will accept that I have a right to see my daughter."

For all his bravado, Nathan was starting to crumble inside at the thought of losing Kelly and becoming a part-time father at best or a non-existent father at worst. Only time would tell. He had to push back the tears which threatened to tumble out of his eyes. He had his pride and didn't want Amanda to witness his vulnerability.

"I'm going out. I need to walk for a bit. Don't wait up. "

Once the door closed, Amanda remained in her seat for a while, numb and destabilised until a little voice called out to her from down the corridor.

"Mummy, Mummy, you've been talking to Daddy for ages. I want a story, please."

"I'm coming Kelly, I'm coming."

Nothing like a child's demands to pull a parent out of their daily grind.

How am I going to explain that to her? Nathan moving out of the flat won't be easy for Kelly to accept. I'll have to make sure I'm around more, at least in the next few weeks. How am I going to juggle this with work? Gosh, this is a mess and it's draining.

She thought of asking Reine to help out especially if, as she'd suspected earlier, she was required to assist the police in the case of the missing young boy. Her instincts were telling her that she would soon hear from the detective in charge. She welcomed the challenge and the chance to find the boy, but cursed the timing of it with Nathan moving out shortly.

Kelly was waiting in the doorway of her room, holding Dolly, looking so young and vulnerable in her pink nightdress with the purple and white unicorn, that Amanda's heart felt a pinch at the news she had to tell her. How can Nathan not want to spend time with such a sweet, gorgeous child? When she had become a mother, the child had taken over her heart, her mind and her soul. She had been devoted to Kelly and always would be. She hated the idea of ever being without her daughter. Compassion for Nathan rose inside her at the thought that the man who fathered Kelly would no longer be part of her daily life. But then again he had had the opportunity to see her every day for the last eight years but had made different choices.

The picture of the missing boy popped into her head, prompting her to wonder what agony his parents were going through again tonight. She had the same sinking feeling now as she'd had when she saw the news flash on TV earlier on. How do parents cope with a missing child, knowing that there was a strong chance the child may not come back alive? It didn't bear thinking about. Kelly's recent short disappearance had been upsetting enough. No way would she be able to deal with the same situation and she wondered how Nathan would fare given the same circumstances too.

After talking to Kelly about Nathan's forthcoming move, answering her questions and soothing her tears, Amanda managed to get her to fall asleep by rocking her in her arms for a while. Yes, she would definitely ask Reine to come down for a few weeks if she was able to as she was not working at the moment. Amanda was convinced that there was no-one better than Grandma Reine to be there for the distraught child. She would calm her and reassure her during the next difficult weeks, until a suitable routine was worked out.

Every night Amanda reflected on the good in her life. Tonight she experienced a more intense gratitude for Kelly, Reine and the people she loved, including Nathan. She did love him, and always would. After all, he had given her Kelly, the most precious person in her life.

KAREN - 2016

[6]

Karen Turner was on her way back from work when she saw the headline about a missing Peckham boy in the newsagent's window. It upset her to read it.

Poor little sod. Poor parents. I can't imagine what they must be going through.

As the boy was from around here, it made her think of her son, Sam who was now sixteen. She thought back to him at the same age as the boy on the poster. She had been his main carer from the start although she had not spent much quality time with him. This was mainly due to the lack of help on Ben's part, as he had not been present much since Sam's birth.

Why on earth did I go and fall in love with Ben Warnham? I still don't know. Mind you, he did look hot compared to the other losers at school. But why him? Talk about being unlucky, falling pregnant at seventeen. That was such a rough time, having a child at that age and raising him mostly on my own. Good job my parents helped, especially when I had to find a job. Give them their due. But I can't believe Sam was only 4 months when I went to work. It was much too soon, I've missed so much of his childhood. But frankly I couldn't stand my parents' moaning any longer. Their moaning about how much money they spent on bills, how much noise Sam was making, on and on. It was driving me bonkers. Gosh, what about their endless comments on Ben? They'd warned me about him and he wasn't welcome in the house. It didn't matter anyway coz Ben wasn't interested in visiting his son. I'm glad I managed to get a council flat a few months later. What a stroke of luck when my cousin told me to get on to the council's list. I loved my little flat, just me and Sam living together.

Karen had managed to get a part-time job in a little café where she was allowed to bring Sam with her until he had gone to nursery three days a week. The other two days, her parents had looked after the toddler. Just as well, as Ben was still unwilling to help raise Sam. An occasional walk in the park with her and Sam, or a quick visit to her flat to chat for fifteen minutes every four months, had been Ben's level of interest in his son. When Sam had gone to school, she had worked longer hours.

After Sam turned eight, Ben took a bit more of an interest in him. He had got himself a flat where, for the first time, Sam was able to stay overnight with her permission. There was no legal agreement between them as to visitation rights. She knew Ben had parental rights but neither one had sought to make any formal agreement between them. However, with his newly found interest in fatherhood, Ben brought with him an arsenal of deplorable parenting ideas.

I should have known Ben getting involved would be bad news. Who lets a child of eight watch horror movies? If Sam hadn't let slip he watched horror films with his dad, I wouldn't even know about it. I tell Ben to stop 'til I'm blue in the face but he couldn't care less. Ben does what he wants, and that's so bloody infuriating. Can't he understand the damage it might cause to Sam? Isn't there a reason why these films are marked Certificate 18? I'm not sure I'll ever get through to Ben. He still lets him watch the movies and worse too, he feeds him junk food every time they're together. Then Sam comes home after seeing him and he's all hyper and I'm the one who has to deal with it. I wish this idiot would listen for once. Frankly, I preferred it when Ben wasn't on the scene. It was tough yes, but at least I made the decisions and he didn't interfere. Sometimes you have to be careful what you wish for."

When Sam hit ten, he started exhibiting disturbing behaviour. She was still embarrassed and deeply ashamed when remembering how neighbours had come to tell her that her son had been seen tormenting two cats in the neighbourhood. Not only that, but the cats had now disappeared without a trace. When she'd questioned Sam, he said he'd been near the cats a few times but he didn't know where they were. Karen was not buying this, but she didn't push, preferring to believe whatever Sam told her rather than causing a conflict. She hated confrontations and avoided them like the plague, since hearing her parents argue with each other on a daily basis. It had gone on for years.

A few months later, an even more alarming incident took place at the swimming pool. For reasons of his own, Sam had grabbed one of his classmates during a swimming lesson, and held her head under the water. The swimming teacher, Mr Simmons, had intervened quickly, and told Karen afterwards that, from Sam's expression on his face, there was little doubt that he had not been larking around. Karen was mortified and found it hard to believe what he'd done. What if he'd drowned her?

She'd asked him this question that night. "Sam, didn't you think that the girl might drown? What went through your thick head? I can't even begin to imagine why you did that? Talk to me Sam. Why did you try to drown Aimee?"

"It's not that bad. She didn't drown, did she?

He had played the big man, arrogant and blasé about what he'd done. But looking at his mother's displeased face, he had burst out crying, apologising to Karen, and showing a degree of remorse.

Well, he's apologised, he's clearly sorry. But I don't understand this child. Why harm the girl? His behaviour is hard to handle. I can't stand it when I see what he does. I feel lost but I have too much on my plate to dwell on this. The boy has to make mistakes to learn from them, doesn't he? I work two jobs to put food on the table and a roof over our heads. Surely, that's more important than digging into Sam's emotions. He is sorry, so that's the end of this.

Given the seriousness of the incident, Sam had been suspended from school for a week. To top it all, social services had come and talked to her about Sam's behaviour. She had confessed to them that she was finding his behaviour at home frustrating, challenging and overwhelming as he never followed instructions, was constantly fidgeting and was generally defiant. The school, in turn, confirmed that he had been disruptive in class, blurting out inappropriate comments, at inappropriate times during the lessons. His homework was not done or, at best, done to a poor standard and he was clearly falling behind his peers. This is when it was agreed to test Sam for Attention Deficit Hyperactivity Disorder (ADHD). On the strength of the results, the school had formally diagnosed Sam as suffering from ADHD.

Karen was given advice on how to moderate his behaviour and his less-than sociable habits. It involved giving him medication daily, spending a lot of time with him and monitoring what he ate. She had tried but, after a week, it proved impossible to devote that much time to Sam and the "healthier" food cost too much money. She was advised to find an activity that Sam would be happy to focus on. He loved all the social media and he decided to get his personal channel on YouTube and do short video clips. Where he got the idea from, she didn't know, but he started talking about the video games that he was playing. His favourite was 'Slender Man', a tall faceless man who stalked young children. In his video clips, Sam commented on what was happening in the games he played.

She had thought the troubles were behind her. When Sam was twelve though, while turning the mattress over in his bed, she found a paraphernalia of blades and scissors with antiseptic wipes in a tin box. She knew some teenagers self-harmed and, in view of the content of the tin box, she wondered if

Sam did. She racked her brain for clues that her assumption was correct. She had remembered that, a few months ago, before making that discovery, Sam's towel in the bathroom had had blood stains on it. He had told Karen it was due to a nosebleed, and she had not paid more attention to it. Come to think of it, that summer, and most of the summers after that, she had rarely seen him in shorts, even when the weather had been hot. She remembered because it was the year of a heatwave, all the weirder for Sam to wear jeans throughout. She felt a bit guilty that she hadn't asked him about it.

What do you expect though? Why the hell would I ask more questions and give myself another headache? Sam is a hard kid to raise and I'm doing my best. I do nothing other than work. I work thirteen bloody hours a day, six days a week. I'm still young and don't even have time to myself. I don't go out. I'll speak to Ben when he next shows up.

She had hoped a talk between father and son might enlighten both parents as to the reason why Sam was self-harming. Ben had been elusive and of little use. Shrugging the whole thing off, Ben convinced her that it would pass, and that the boy had to toughen up anyway.

A couple of years later, she noticed Sam's behaviour was getting stranger. He appeared spaced out every time he came back from Ben's and often in the evening too, when he was at home. She knew Ben had been smoking cannabis for several years. She had an uneasy suspicion he was sharing his habit with Sam. It would be farfetched to most parents, but Karen knew better. She wouldn't put it past Ben to encourage his off-spring, aged fourteen, to partake in weed smoking. Ben believed that all the bad publicity was just a whole lot of cobblers. He was convinced that people who denigrated the drug knew nothing. After all, he, Ben, was the expert. Ben's sheer arrogance and ignorance had always astonished Karen.

She had often made it her mission to talk to Sam about giving up cannabis, but each time he had fobbed her off. One day he had pushed her roughly away from him to get out of the house when she had once again broached the subject. His behaviour was getting more and more erratic, even aggressive on several occasions. His schoolwork was suffering badly. He now spent most of his time in his room, becoming more and more addicted to even weirder video games or spending time writing computer games. He had a knack for understanding the complexities of Information Technology. Inside of her, Karen was proud of his ability to write software. She understood little about the internet, even less about video games and nothing at all about computer coding and software. Karen had no idea either that there was such a thing as parental controls on a computer to ensure children stay safe from on-line predators. This was a world that Karen had no concept of, or any idea about. She just spent her life going from home to one job then to the other and back home again. No-one around her had mentioned the fact that, as Sam's mother, internet safety fell under her area of responsibility. Ben certainly hadn't told her anything about it and neither had Sam.

Right now, she was weary after a long day. She was not sure why, but Sam had changed. At best his behaviour had got even stranger and at worst downright challenging. The last few years had become a real nightmare for her. She was now a thirty-something, overworked, single mother, at her wits end with both Sam and Ben.

Her low income had never allowed her to move away from Peckham, not the most salubrious area to raise a kid in. Her dad had passed away five years ago. She had left her council flat to go and live in her mother's house with Sam. It had been trying when her mother had suffered with dementia the last two years of her life.

Another burden I had to carry at the time. As if I hadn't had enough on my plate with a useless man and a difficult son. My goodness! I never want to go through such hard times again.

She was engrossed in her thoughts and had reached home without realising it. On opening the front door, a familiar smell assaulted her nose.

"Sam! Get down here, what are you smoking again? Get your arse down here now."

A skinny, dark haired teenager was looking down at her from the top of the stairs, an arrogant smile on his face, shrugging his shoulders.

"Oh shut the fuck up stupid woman. Nag, nag, nag… It's only a bit of weed. I need a smoke to relax after school and to put up with your moaning all the time. What's your problem? Dad's okay with it. Leave me alone will you."

She heard the door slam behind Sam as he walked back into his bedroom. She was pissed-off with him talking to her like this. But she was too scared to confront him. To be honest, she was often intimidated by Sam. When he was high, he had a dead look in his eyes that frightened her. She decided not to push this recurring argument about cannabis smoking. Instead, Karen cursed the day Ben had taken more interest in Sam.

Why didn't this loser let us be? What's happening to Sam? This is all that jerk's fault. Sam can't accept there is anything wrong with his dad and I always end up being the villain. I am sick to the back teeth of this.

Inside she was fuming, but she knew better than to waste her breath talking to Ben about it. The man was convinced that he was right. She had never seen any humility in Ben Warnham.

Karen had first noticed Ben at school when she was nearly fifteen and he was sixteen. She had the hots for him from the start. She had done her best to catch his attention. But Ben had spent the next two years ignoring her, parading in the neighbourhood with bimbos who were happy to sleep with him, and defying the school rules whenever possible. He did have a certain rough charm. His rebel appearance and behaviour attracted quite a few members of the opposite sex. She was so infatuated with him that her years at school had been as miserable as sin. It had been even worse after he'd left school to do a car mechanic apprenticeship. She missed him being at school for her final years. Then one day, he walked into the McDonalds where she was working at weekends. For whatever reason, he had started to chat her up. He had finally looked at her. Only to charm her into sleeping with him.

It just shows you how naïve and stupid I was. I believed everything he told me. He was a smooth talker back then. He got me believing him when he said he had fancied me for years and he was waiting until I was older. He even said he loved me and wanted to go out with me. I was so gullible. How did I fall for the usual "If you love me, you'll sleep with me."

She had lost her virginity to him one night at his place, when his parents were out of the house. She had been incredulous that her own parents did not allow her to have boys over, even her new boyfriend.

This is the twentieth century for God's sake. Crazy, old fashioned people.

When she found out she was pregnant after five months of going out with Ben, he scarpered at the news of the pregnancy. When he'd heard she had given birth to a baby boy, he came to see her to make sure the child was normal. After that, he proved to be the elusive father her parents had warned her about. She felt sorry that Sam had entered the world without a father to greet him and be there for him.

She was thankful her mother, June, was no longer alive to see how Sam was behaving now. When June had started showing signs of dementia, Sam had only been thirteen, and luckily she had not noticed his change of behaviour. To be fair, he had been mindful of his grandmother. It had been a rough couple of years as June was constantly leaving the house, roaming around the neighbourhood. Karen had had CCTV cameras installed to keep an eye on her mother as she often wandered off. At least she would know in which direction to start her search. She missed her mother, but it was a relief that the pressure of caring for her had eased.

"Mum, what's for dinner? I'm hungry. Get dinner done will you, I need to go out soon."

"Sam, don't talk to me that way. I just got in and I'm tired. Cook your own food. Where are you going anyway? It is a school night and I want you back here by nine. Got it?"

She hated it when Sam was rude to her and she didn't like him going out at night either. She never knew where he was going and did not feel confident enough to stop him. This was another area where she proved to be a weak mother as Sam rarely came back at the given time. She hoped the next couple of years would pass as quickly as possible. She wished that he would leave home, and that she did not have to deal with him anymore.

She walked up the stairs as an angry Sam was coming down to the kitchen to prepare his food. She tried to kiss him when they were level, but he pushed her back roughly and sped down the stairs. Her feelings hurt, she went past Sam's room to go to her bedroom. His door was open. The heavy smell of weed lingering in the room made her nauseous. She walked in to open the window but felt more unsettled when she glanced at the computer screen. She was sickened by the menacing image of 'Slender Man', surrounded by dead children, displayed on the screen. From the corner of her eye, she caught a glimpse of something sticking out slightly from under Sam's bed.

"What the heck is this? Sam, Sam... Come back up here right now."

In the kitchen, Sam ignored her, he was tired of hearing his mother moan and have a go at him. She was uncool and a real pain in the arse. As far back as he could remember he had resented his mother for working all the time. For not doing stuff with him when he was a kid. He resented her the most for what he perceived as her failure to ensure his father was permanently in his life. To him, Ben was a cool dude even though he was absent more than Sam would have liked. None of his mates at school had dads who watched horror movies with them when they were kids. Certainly, none of his mates had dads who shared their stash of cannabis with their kid. Sam's dad did. That had been cool. Sam had never expected that.

They had gone to see a mate of his, a guy named Josh, and that was the first time Sam had been aware that his dad smoked cannabis. Ben had bought a big bag of it from Josh in full view of his son. That evening at his flat Ben had smoked a joint and, seeing Sam's inquisitive look, he had passed it to him to try. It was horrible at first because the joint smelled funny. He had never smoked tobacco and he didn't know how to inhale. He had just puffed on the joint in a way that had made Ben laugh at him and tease him. His head had started to spin like mad and he was nauseous. Ben had mocked him, saying he'd turned as green as the cartoon character Shrek.

What do I care? That Shrek cartoon is stupid anyway. It's for little kids. Who wants to watch an ugly green monster? I'm not a child anymore. This Disney rubbish is for sissies and am not one of them. I like horror films with real people getting killed and tortured. The stuff Dad has shown me since I was little.

He remembered how at first he had been shit-scared and refused to sleep without the light on in the corridor. He had nightmares after the first few movies, but the more he had watched horror films with his dad, the more he had found them fascinating. He'd felt a growing desire to be like the characters he admired in his favourite films. But he had been young then and now he was obsessed with 'Slender Man'. That dude was a cool character. He had no face, he was tall, stick thin and the best part of the game was when 'Slender Man' was stalking kids in the woods. The fear showed on their faces. Sam's heart always beat faster when their fear was tangible. It gave him a sense of power over them as he was playing the game. His mum was always bugging him to play something different or to focus on his schoolwork. Sam ignored her as usual.

I hate bloody school. All the other kids are idiots. They wanna act like adults but they know nothing. Just like that div, Aimee. She made me mad, the little bitch, laughing at me. Just coz she's got a posh car, posh clothes and lives in a posh house. Man, did I love putting her ugly face in the water at the swimming pool. Serves her right, stuck up bitch. But because of her, the school now treats me like a retard. I swear, she's gonna pay for this one way or another, if it fucking kills me!

AMANDA - 2016

[7]

Amanda had been right. Sixty hours after the news broke about the missing Peckham boy, she received a call from Robert Denton, the Chief Superintendent at the police station she had been visiting on the day of Kelly's brief disappearance.

The presentation she had done at the Southwark police station to several Chief Inspectors had been useful. The word had gone around about the two cases she had solved. Amanda King was a psychic medium deemed to be a useful resource to be contacted in cases which were stalling.

She was getting ready to take Kelly to school when the phone rang. Amanda was a bit pushed for time. She had hoped Reine would come down to help out with Kelly when Nathan moved out, but she had not been able to. Reine was expected in the next few weeks.

Amanda had a hunch that the call was not good news. She was undecided whether to answer it or let the answering machine pick it up. Somehow she knew she had to take the call.

"Kelly, finish getting ready by yourself. I need to see who is calling. We'll go in a few minutes. Okay sweetheart?"

Kelly ran back into her room to put on her school shoes. On the way, she picked a pink hair crunchy.

"Hello, may I speak to Amanda please. My name is Robert Denton."

"Speaking. Good morning, Robert. Good to hear from you."

"Hi Amanda, I'm glad you're home. I need to speak to you urgently, do you have a minute please?"

"Well I need to take my daughter to school in ten minutes, but I can talk for a bit. What can I do for you?"

Robert Denton had been asked to contact her to request her help. Denton informed her that since Jamie Wilson's disappearance, three nights ago, the detectives in charge of the case at Peckham police station had not come up with enough information to find him. As mentioned on the news, the boy had left his home, unnoticed, at around 11.30 pm, carrying five video games in a small rucksack and had not been seen since. Detectives had looked at the computer the boy kept in his bedroom. They had found out that he had a Facebook account. It seemed that he had been in contact with other fans of Xbox video games via a public group called "XBoys."

Looking through the conversations on Jamie's Facebook wall and on the "XBoys" group, it was clear that he'd had several exchanges recently with a user called 'Scream face'. They had agreed to meet on the night Jamie had disappeared. The detectives had not found out where the meeting had taken place nor who the other boy or person was. The computer's IP address of 'Scream face' was identified but it had not led anywhere specific enough to either locate him or identify him. Even going through the internet provider, the investigation team weren't able to pinpoint who or where 'Scream face' was. The police even visited pawnshops in the area, in case they had been offered cheap games similar to the ones Jamie had taken with him. They had hoped to get a small lead by now, but the search had turned up nothing so far.

"Amanda, we need your help. Would you be willing to go to Peckham police station today to speak to my colleague, Detective Chief Inspector

Andrew Gates, and work with his team to find out where the boy might be, please?"

"Yes, of course, I'll go and meet him once Kelly is at school and take it from there."

"Thank you, Amanda. We all want this case solved urgently and we hope you can help us crack it. We have to find the boy. It has been too long already, please do what you can to assist Andrew Gates. I'll speak to you soon. Bye Amanda."

"I understand the urgency and will do my best. Bye Robert."

Half an hour later, having dropped off Kelly at school, and confirmed with Andrew Gates that he was available, Amanda then made her way to Peckham police station. She was shown promptly to the Chief Inspector's office.

Andrew Gates, a pleasant looking, slightly rotund man, greeted her with a warm smile and a firm handshake. He had a faint Scottish accent. Amanda noticed the rather old-fashioned hair style which wasn't quite congruent with the handsome face.

"Ms King, nice to meet you. Thank you for taking the time to come in today."

"Hello, Detective Chief Inspector. Nice to meet you too. Please call me Amanda. Are there any updates on what Chief Superintendent Denton told me?"

"Robert Denton is up to speed. He probably told you everything we know for now. We are keen to solve this case and find the boy but, in all honesty, we have drawn a blank. Realistically, I think we are looking for a body now. We didn't find Jamie in the first forty eight hours and from experience, I think we are more likely to find him dead than alive. I am hoping you are able to locate him and bring answers to us and to his distraught parents."

"I will do my best to help."

"I've asked Jamie's parents to give us a recent photo of the boy and a toy of his. I understand that's what you need to work? Is that right?"

"Yes, that's correct. Thank you. I felt the need to help the minute I heard the news on TV four days ago. May I sit in a quiet room with the photo and the toy and see what I can come up with."

"Sure, Ms King, eh sorry, Amanda. Please follow me."

Since seeing the news on TV, Amanda had experienced a sense of foreboding whenever she thought of the boy. That had intensified after speaking to Denton that morning. She wasn't sure yet, but she suspected what the outcome of this investigation would be. At this precise moment, she felt like thousands of ice-cold water jets were being directed at her spine. Very unsettling indeed. She followed Andrew Gates into a room and thanked him. She sat down, relaxed and grounded herself while looking at the photo and the object she was holding.

Despite the dilemma being a gifted young child had caused her, she was absolutely certain that helping the police now was her purpose in life, bringing much needed answers and closure in devastating situations. She once again thanked the universe for her gift and focussed on the picture of the young boy. He was smiling, showing two front teeth missing, which gave him a bit of a clown look. He had a round face and longish brown hair. His eyes were a piercing blue which she had rarely seen in anyone. The thought "he was such a beautiful boy", came unbidden to the forefront of her consciousness. She noticed the "was."

The way Amanda worked was to focus first on a photo of the missing person/victim to get a sense of his/her energy and to connect with the soul. Often she would see brief glimpses of the person in happier times. This was because the spirits showed themselves as a reflection of the love that person had in their heart as well as their physical appearance. After connecting with the soul, whilst holding the person's belonging, she often got more information on what had happened to them, in the form of short clips - as she had explained to Kelly a few nights back.

Today, holding a Buzz Lightyear toy belonging to Jamie, she saw him as a spirit in happier times and that was her confirmation that he had passed already. Next she saw a fairly large house, looking like a guesthouse, near a road junction with sign posts to Herne Hill and Tulse Hill. It appeared faintly familiar to her. She had to focus to recognise the location of the building. She had a flash of broken doors, several bedrooms with boarded windows, and an overgrown garden. It appeared to her that this was a disused guesthouse. She had not seen where the body of the boy was exactly, but she knew with certainty that the police would find him in one of the bedrooms. She had a vague sensation of seeing somebody of average height, sauntering from room to room, carrying a little blue rucksack with a red motif, and then leaving the house through one of the ground floor windows. The boarding had been kicked in. She focussed hard to see the face of the intruder but only saw a mask. A strange mask she had seen before. It was white, long and distorted, with a strange shaped mouth and weird slanted, all dark, unseeing eyes. Where had she seen that mask? There was no time to think about this further though.

She had to tell the detectives about what she'd

seen as the intruder might be the killer. She rushed out of the room, reached Andrew Gates' office, her words coming out fast, eager to relate what her brain had seen.

"Jamie is dead, Andrew. He is in a disused guesthouse. It's boarded up and near the junction of two roads leading to Tulse Hill and Herne Hill. I saw a person leaving the house. I am convinced it is a male, average height, slim, wearing a strange mask. I've seen the mask before but not sure where. It is white long and distorted…"

"Might be from the film 'Scream'. The mask matches your description and remember the Facebook name of the person meeting Jamie was 'Scream face'. I'll bring it up on my computer and you can tell me if that's what you saw. Here it is. Is that the one Amanda?"

"Oh my God, yes, it is. I knew I had seen it before, but I didn't remember where. Chief Inspector please can you tell me the colour of the rucksack Jamie was carrying that night?"

"Let me see, it says here that Jamie was carrying a blue rucksack with a Spiderman motif on it. I assume it would be mainly blue and red, why?"

"I saw the person I assume to be the killer carry the rucksack. He was still holding it when he left the site through a window on the ground floor. My instinct tells me he's the killer. How can you find the location of it? I think I know where it is but can't pinpoint it. The South Circular comes to my mind, I've driven there many times and that's why it's familiar I think."

"Okay, let me call the detective in charge for him to update the team on what you saw and get a search organised. Please take a seat whilst I speak to my colleagues. Can I get a tea or a coffee brought to you?"

"No thanks, Andrew."

As Andrew picked up the phone on his desk, Amanda sunk back into the chair, feeling apprehension at whether they would find the location.

"Hello, Gary, it's Andrew. I have new information on Jamie's disappearance. Amanda the psychic medium is certain that his body …. Yes she said his body… I know, Gary. We were hoping he was alive, but it is highly likely he is dead already. Please get your guys working as quickly as possible on finding a disused guesthouse with a garden, windows boarded up at a junction of two roads, possibly on the South Circular, one going to Herne Hill and the other to Tulse Hill. Keep me posted and get cracking, the murderer may have just left the place. We need to get there ASAP. One last thing, Gary. When you know the location of the house, get a car for me and Amanda to go to the place with your officers."

As he ended the conversation, Andrew turned to Amanda with an enquiring look. He was about to go to the incident room, but suddenly had a thought.

"If we come up with an address quickly, would you be able to come with us to confirm we have identified the location you saw?"

"Yes, I can. I usually pick up my daughter from school at three o'clock. If I'm still with you then, I will need to line up a sitter to pick her up."

The investigation room was buzzing with activity when Andrew Gates walked in. He looked over the information flashing on the computers as his team worked to identify the location of the house. He knew it might take a little while. He was eager to go to the place the minute it was identified, to get clues on the murderer and to recover Jamie's body if indeed he was dead as Amanda had perceived. He felt sadness shroud his heart. He had been in this business for eighteen years, but it never got any easier when the victim was a child. It still made him upset. He guessed that not being blasé about it gave him an extra incentive to go after the killer and put him behind bars.

"Gary, any updates yet?"

Andrew was fidgety, eager to find the guesthouse

and Jamie. He did not relish telling the parents that Jamie's body had been found. He would have much rather informed them their little boy was alive. Although the boy had been missing for longer than the critical forty-eight hours, he had hoped not to have to inform another set of parents of their child's death. He might not get his wish. He had no choice but to wait patiently. A result finally came forty minutes later.

"Boss, we've got it. It is on the South Circular, just outside Dulwich. The house has been abandoned for almost a year. It's called "The Junction Guesthouse." We've a car at the front for you, me and Ms King. I have despatched two detectives to the guesthouse and a team of SOCOs (Scene of Crime Officers)."

Putting his jacket on, the detective in charge, Bill Wyatt, turned to Andrew Gates, as he was making his way towards the door.

"You coming boss? Are you getting the medium or shall I?"

"Go ahead. I'll meet you by the car with her."

Andrew Gates rushed back to his office, eager and apprehensive to get to the location and find clues to identify the killer. He did not normally attend crime scenes. But due to the unusual way they had obtained their information about Jamie's whereabouts, Andrew felt his presence alongside Amanda was necessary.

Thanks to Amanda, they were aware of the mask and that the killer had kept the little rucksack. His mind was going around thinking about the identity of the murderer. He had enough experience and common sense to know that, until he got to the scene and his men started running forensic tests, it was pointless making assumptions.

"We have a location. Let's go! A car is waiting for us at the front. You were right, it is on the South Circular near Dulwich."

In the car, the silence from the detectives and from Amanda was ominous. The men were focussing on the task ahead and Amanda was preparing herself for another harrowing sight. She had not seen the exact location of Jamie's body in the house, but she had a certainty in her heart that he had been harmed before being killed. She had sensed this from the time she heard the news on the TV. She had connected with him, his distress and pain. She knew what awaited them at the crime scene would not be a pretty sight.

Speeding to the crime scene in the police car, it felt unreal to Amanda, although somewhat reassuring, to be working for the police. Almost as if it would give her, and hers a protective cloak. They arrived at the guesthouse within ten minutes and Amanda saw a police car had already arrived. Getting out of the car, Amanda nodded to Andrew Gates's questioning look.

"Yes. This is the house I saw. The killer left through that window here on the ground floor. I think Jamie is in one of the ground floor bedrooms. Do you want me to go in with you or shall I wait here?"

"That's okay, Amanda. You have confirmed that this is the house you saw. I'm grateful you led us to this location. Thank you. My men are going in to check where the body is. I think it's better for you to wait outside until we get confirmation that we have found Jamie, but if you prefer to leave now the driver will take you back to the station to get your car."

"No, I'll wait here and see if you have found Jamie before being driven back to the station."

"Ok. Just sit in the car and I'll come back to you shortly."

* * *

This incident had heightened Amanda's level of apprehension with regards to Kelly's safety in a world where vile acts were committed regularly on children. Sitting alone in the back of the police car, she decided it was wiser for her not to witness what Jamie had endured during his ordeal. Andrew Gates had told her he would update her on what they had found. She would learn soon enough what fate little Jamie had met. She noticed that quite a few people had assembled to see why a number of policemen and detectives were going in and out of the guest house. The inquisitive crowd parted to let a small van with darkened windows pull up behind the police car. Amanda had seen this type of vehicle before. It was the van sent by the coroner's office, should they find Jamie's body. Her heart felt heavy and she wished the outcome could have been different.

[8]

Nathan sat down on the worn-out, uncomfortable sofa, weary after a horrid day working for Josh. Either the tenants were getting worse or Josh was a bad landlord. Nathan had had complaint after complaint from the tenants and refusals to pay the rent or any arrears. One had been mad enough to nearly attack Nathan this morning. Only the threat of calling the police got the tenant to calm down.

Christ! What a job! As if life isn't hard enough living in this poxy, small flat. It's badly equipped, gloomy and uncomfortable. I know beggars can't be choosers and I'm grateful to Josh, but it's not like being at home with the family. I miss home, I miss Kelly and I miss Amanda, even her nagging.

At times he struggled still to comprehend why he had to leave the family home because of what

Amanda saw as his shortcomings. She'd not acknowledged the fact he was a man and his job was his purpose in life. A relationship was never the top priority for a man. Nathan made allowance for it in his life, but Amanda had failed to understand relationships were of a different importance to a man than to a woman.

He got up to pour himself a drink. A stiff scotch would erase the hassle of the day and help him face the loneliness of the evening, the emptiness of the place and his yearning to see his daughter. The silence was getting him down. He turned on the old TV Josh had left for him. The evening news was on. A senior police officer was holding a press conference. Behind him was the picture of the boy Nathan remembered seeing in the news recently. It was the young boy who had gone missing the night Amanda told him he had to move out. Intrigued, he turned the volume up and sat back down, his drink in his hand.

"Today, we've unfortunately found the body of the missing boy, Jamie Wilson, in a disused guesthouse. This case is now classified as a homicide and we are appealing to anyone for information. Jamie was stabbed several times and sexually molested. The attack was vicious and we are appealing to anyone aware of a man or a boy, medium height, in possession of a 'Scream mask'. He may have been seen in the Peckham, Dulwich and Herne Hill area on September 17th or a few days after Jamie went missing. We need to identify the killer. Someone in the area is bound to be aware that one of their relatives or friends may have such a mask or may match the description. I urge anyone to come forward with any information. This person is dangerous and is not to be approached by members of the public. Any sighting or information is to be reported to the investigation team. Finally, I want to appeal directly to the person responsible for Jamie's murder to come forward and hand himself in.

Jamie's parents have asked me to thank the public for the messages of sympathy they have received from the local community. They are asking to be allowed to grieve in peace and come to terms with the tragic loss of their son. Thank you."

On the TV screen, journalists scrambled to ask more questions, but the Detective Inspector had walked away from the conference, not intending to answer them. Nathan was saddened by the fate Jamie had encountered. He was shocked that people were capable of killing others, especially children.

I don't get it. What on earth leads a human being to kill another one in such a vicious way? What goes through the mind of a killer? I've always wondered what turns a perfectly ordinary human into a murderer.

He had watched a documentary recently about Britain's deadliest kids. He had got an answer to his question. However, he had been surprised to hear that certain people are born with certain genetic traits, making them predisposed to killing if this particular gene got activated. One of the experts had explained that major stress and emotional situations like bullying at school, abuse, social isolation often caused the activation of the gene. This had made Nathan wonder how many people in this world carried the killing trait in their gene pool, and whether the worst crimes against humanity were down to that killing gene.

I bet the media will now blame the killer's mother for what he did to little Jamie. I don't know why they often do that. I remember many cases where the crime committed by the kid was put down to the lack of love and interaction with the mother. It's always intrigued me how the mother is blamed even though, in a lot of cases, the father is absent. Christ, am I gonna be an absent father too? This is all wrong. I feel sorry for mothers of criminals. Imagine hearing about the vile acts your flesh and blood committed. It must be devastating. Do they ever recover from the stigma, I wonder?

Being interested in TV documentaries on famous

crimes, Nathan had wondered what it must like to be the mother of the Yorkshire ripper who had killed thirteen women over many years. Or imagine being the mother of Dennis Nilsen who had killed twelve men, dismembered their bodies and either burnt parts of their bodies or flushed them down the toilet. He would love to know what they had felt when hearing that their children had committed such monstrous acts.

He thought that sucked. In his mind, the whole of society was responsible when a human being committed a heinous crime, especially if the victim was a child or if the killer was also a child. But his way of thinking had got him into trouble during discussions with work colleagues or friends. For that reason, he tended to keep his opinions to himself on this subject. Right now he felt extreme sympathy for Jamie's parents. The thought of his precious daughter ever getting harmed turned the blood coursing through his veins into freezing water.

Remembering Amanda's reaction on the night the boy had disappeared, he wondered if she had assisted the police in finding Jamie. He was glad the family knew what'd happened to their boy. Most probably thanks to Amanda using the gift he had often sniggered at! He had discovered early on after their initial meeting that Amanda had psychic gifts.

He had laughed and teased her frequently throughout their time together. He had not been into spiritual things at all, being a practical type. On occasions, he had even played childish tricks on her such as hiding her stuff, telling her to visualise where it was. At first it had been a bit of fun. But the novelty had worn off for Amanda and the constant comments and teasing had no longer been welcome.

Since she'd solved two missing person cases in the last year, and possibly this one, he found himself admiring her more and respecting what she did. He wished he had shown her more respect and admiration when they were still together.

Still having some work to do, Nathan focussed his attention on his brother and his business. Josh was a closed book when it came to talking about his numerous businesses. That reluctance gave Nathan the impression his brother indulged in activities which were not always kosher.

Look at his reaction when Kelly went missing. He was furious that I'd brought the cops' attention on myself when I was out collecting his rents. I didn't say anything to the police about what I was doing in the area that afternoon. As rent collecting is legal, it's gotta be that some of his tenants are illegal. It's the only way I can explain his over-reacting.

It wasn't just with the property rental business

that Nathan questioned his brother's integrity and morality. He'd come across a number of people traipsing to Josh's office on a regular basis to buy cannabis. It was illegal and he wondered where his brother was getting his supply from. He knew that Josh had various contacts abroad and went on extended long haul trips several times a year. Nathan was not against cannabis smoking but did not indulge in it himself. He'd seen first-hand how a couple of his peers at school had been affected mentally after smoking the stuff every day for years. He wanted better for himself. He was health conscious and treated his body with respect. He was troubled by the fact that his brother was, to all intent and purposes, a drug dealer. That a member of his family encouraged others to use drugs did not sit well with him.

He'd not been impressed either when he'd seen a mate of Josh, a few months back, coming in with his teenage kid to buy cannabis. From the guy's attitude, it was obvious he thought there was nothing wrong with smoking weed. He'd even implied he shared his stash with his sixteen year-old son.

That's bloody ludicrous. It's hard enough for kids to resist pressure from their mates not to get into drugs. What kind of a father encourages his kid to smoke weed? That guy, Ben Warnham, I think his name was, looked a right loser. I feel sorry for the boy and God knows what the future holds for this kid.

Nathan had been a bit wild as a teenager and young adult. He had been neither a great son, nor a great boyfriend to Amanda in his youth. He used to drink a bit too much at parties, but one thing he had never done, was to indulge in drugs. He was proud of himself as it had often been challenging to resist temptation, especially when he hadn't fitted in with his peers. Yet, he had resisted doing the wrong thing to gain a false sense of belonging.

My goodness, I'm in a gloomy mood tonight. I'm gonna call Amanda. It's not that late. I want to speak to Kelly. I want to hear my girl's silly jokes and sweet voice and know that the world is okay and all is well.

Having decided to ring, he felt in lighter spirit and picked up his mobile.

"Hi Amanda, it's me. Listen, sorry, I know it's a bit late, but I want to speak to Kelly. I miss her. I've had a shit day and I want to hear her voice. Please let me speak to her."

"She is in the bath, Nathan but she'll be out soon. It's a school night, she needs to go to bed but you can have ten minutes with her."

"Thanks, Amanda. I saw the news tonight. I meant to ask you about that kid that went missing and they found dead. That's tragic. Did you help the police find him?"

"Yes, I did, Nathan. I guess my gift is useful after all, eh? It was hard to hear what the killer did to the boy. The police didn't give all the information on the news. It's shocking. I need to speak to somebody about it."

"What happened?"

"You can't discuss what I am telling you with anyone. The detective in charge told me Jamie had been sexually assaulted with a wooden stick. What kind of a sick person can do that to a young kid? I felt ill when they told me. I knew this case would be harrowing, but I never expected to hear this. As if that wasn't enough, he'd been stabbed in various places as if the killer had practised stabbing a dummy. And what's even more incredible, is that the police have no forensic evidence, no DNA and there were no CCTV cameras at or near the guesthouse. The police have checked footage in the vicinity but can't see the masked killer.

I think he must have removed his mask when he left the grounds of the property. I had picked up on the location. I knew Jamie was dead as his spirit came to me, but I was unable to see the face of the killer. Nathan, I can't bear to think about his parents.

I know he is at peace now, but I can't stop thinking about him. What if it had been Kelly?"

Tears had been welling up inside Amanda all day. Talking about what she had heard was a relief. She sobbed and sobbed on the phone. Nathan listened to her distress, unsure how best to help her.

"Listen, I know we're not together anymore but please let me come over. I can be there soon, to read Kelly a story and put her to bed. If she is distracted, she might not see how upset you are. Then we can have a drink and a chat about the case if you want. What do you say? Please let me do this for you and for Kelly."

Amanda didn't have the energy to bear a grudge against Nathan, or hold him at a distance today. After all, she still loved him. She'd dreaded facing Kelly from the moment she'd picked her up from school. She didn't want to worry her but holding back the tears had been challenging. She was tired now and it was harder to pretend that everything was fine.

"Okay. Thanks Nathan. Yes please, come over. I'll tell Kelly you're on your way to see her. Hopefully, she'll be so excited that she won't notice my red eyes. Hurry then, please. See you shortly."

Nathan was happy with this unexpected opportunity to see Kelly. Besides, him being there for Amanda when she was upset, might show her he still cared. It was his chance to prove to her that he was capable of being a reliable partner.

Where there's a will, there's a way. I'm determined to find a way to get Amanda back and to salvage our relationship for the third time. They do say third time lucky, so why not.

He had a grin on his face. He had not felt that happy and light-hearted all day, albeit for weeks. He was still grinning when he got into his car and pulled out of the parking space. In his excitement, he failed to notice a figure walking on the pavement, ahead of him, carrying a little blue and red rucksack out of which peered a white floppy object.

HALLOWEEN - 2016

[9]

"Emergency services, which service do you require?"

"Police please."

"Police emergency."

"We need help. My daughter's friend has been abducted by a creepy male, who's wearing a mask like the guy who killed the boy Jamie. She's only fourteen, you must find her... please you've got to find her before he kills her."

"Sir, please calm down. What is your name? Tell me exactly where the incident took place, and when and who has been abducted."

"My name is Spencer Buckley. It happened about twenty minutes ago, outside the Dulwich Leisure Centre. My daughter Chloe was late to meet her friend Lisa to go trick or treating. When she got there, she saw Lisa walk away down the street with a man wearing a 'Smiley mask'. He was holding her tightly against him, with his arm around her waist. Chloe called out to her, but Lisa ignored her. Or maybe she didn't hear as she carried on walking with the man. My Chloe got scared to go after them because the police had said Jamie's killer is dangerous. She came straight home, told me and I'm calling you now. We tried Lisa's mobile several times, but it goes to voicemail. I wasn't sure whether to call her parents first. They must be informed."

"Alright, Sir. First things first, can I have your address and a police officer will come and talk to your daughter to get a clear description. We'll send a patrol car around the area too but we need to talk to Chloe straightaway. We need the name of the minor who has been allegedly abducted..."

"What do you mean allegedly? Chloe saw her go with a male wearing a mask. It might be Halloween, but she knew what she saw wasn't right. Lisa isn't the type of girl to go with a man and not wait for Chloe. My daughter didn't make that up."

"Sir, we have to assume it's an allegation until we can prove it, or until we have a full statement from Chloe and from Lisa's parents confirming she is missing. Maybe she ran off with a boyfriend that they don't know about. What is your address, Sir?"

"My address is 133 Crystal Palace Road, East Dulwich. The girl is Lisa Palmer, I think she lives near East Dulwich Station. Please hurry. You need to find her before any harm comes to her. She is only fourteen years old, for Christ's sake!"

"Sir, don't worry, an officer will be with you shortly."

The call handler ended the call and passed on the information to the relevant personnel. He wondered about the male wearing a mask. The community had been agitated and scared since September when little Jamie had been found dead. In the weeks since, no progress had been made in finding the killer. This sighting tonight, on Halloween night, may prove to be what the detectives needed to progress the case. Providing both cases were related. He just hoped the girl who had been abducted, if indeed she had been abducted, was not going to meet the same fate as poor Jamie.

This same thought had crossed Lisa's mind as she was walking alongside her abductor for what felt like hours. It was dark. She was scared. She didn't know where they were heading. None of the streets were familiar. She thought her abductor was a teenager because of his voice. He was holding her tight against him and pressing a knife against her ribs to stop her from screaming or saying anything to passers-by.

Surely they noticed her frightened expression, and the scary mask the boy was wearing. Why didn't they say anything? As people on the pavements were coming across the duo, she had heard laughs and comments:

"Look at those two going trick or treating. Great costume. Isn't that mask from a horror film?"

To her dismay, they had merely thought they were dressed up for Halloween. She wanted to scream at them but was petrified he would stab her. A few weeks ago, she'd heard her parents talk about a ten year old boy called Jamie, and that his killer had been wearing a 'Scream mask'. The police had said that person was dangerous and should not be approached. What if it was him?

Maybe I'm wrong. Yes, I must be wrong coz this guy wears a 'Smiley mask' and not a 'Scream mask'. Maybe I'll be alright.

She repeated that thought over and over to soothe her growing fear. They had walked near a railway line. Probably the one going towards London Bridge. That was the only train line she knew around where she lived. She had used it when she'd gone with her parents to the London Dungeon under London Bridge Station. They'd gone to Borough Market many times with her older sister. She liked going to

Borough Market but had often thought it would be cooler to go by herself than with her parents. She was a teenager now after all. She was fourteen, not a baby anymore. Fourteen or not, right now she didn't feel brave. Right now, she'd give anything to be back home with her parents. This boy scared her. She was unable to free herself or run away.

Oh my God. Where is he taking me? What does he want? I'm scared. I want to go home. He said he was a mate of Chloe's on Facebook. I know I was stupid to talk to him. He said he wanted to go trick or treating and I did too. Maybe he's a perv. I hope Chloe saw us. Please God, make sure Chloe saw us. Make her call the police. Please.

She was hanging on to a little seed of hope that Chloe had seen her and had called the police already to report her abduction. She had never prayed as hard as she did right now. If Chloe had called her parents and the police, then they might find her soon. But then another worrying thought took hold of her.

How about my parents? What are they gonna say? They're gonna be furious I was meeting a guy and dead worried. I'm sure I'll be grounded after that. I don't care, I just want to go home. Mum, Dad, please come and get me. This weirdo is scaring me and I am lost. Please don't let him hurt me. Please come and get me.

Usually, Lisa only prayed during school

assemblies, therefore she was not sure if her prayers would be heard. Her survival instinct told her to ask for help anyway.

They had walked in a largely empty park for a little while, then crossed a road over to a dark alley. He suddenly stopped, looked around him as if to find his bearings then pulled her towards a sort of warehouse or garage under a railway arch. It was dilapidated, dark and gloomy with a black door half hanging from its hinges. It looked morbid. She had no idea where she was, but 'Smiley' knew. She called him 'Smiley' as she had no idea what his name was. He'd only said a few words to her since her abduction to tell her to keep quiet or he would stab her and leave her to bleed to death on the pavement. Since that threat, she'd tried to talk to him a little, but he had ignored her questions. He grabbed the door and yanked it open with his right hand, whilst holding her in an arm lock with his left hand. The door was stuck half-way. They squeezed in, one at a time, Lisa now in front of him, to get in the garage. The fear was flooding her trembling body. He pushed her roughly into the scary darkness, then pulled the door to him to close it.

Where are we? Mum, please come and find me. I promise I'll be good all the time.

In the semi-darkness, foul smells assaulted her nostrils; urine, damp, sweat. The disgusting air she was breathing made her gag. She stood, nauseous, quivering with fear, her face drenched with tears. She was ashamed of the urine running down her legs. The sheer fright was chilling her to the core. It felt eerie. The place shook with the rumbling of a train up above. They were under a train line, but where?

If there is a train, there is a station nearby and people around. Someone is bound to find me sooner or later. He can't hide me here for ever. Please, please, somebody come and get me away from this nightmare.

Apart from the occasional coherent thought, she was losing control of her emotions. Her fear was rampant. She was in turn whimpering then sobbing, unable to find the right words to soothe her fear. She had lost all sense of timing and of reality. She just wanted to go home. With the innocence of her fourteen springs, she had never imagined such a nightmare would happen to her. Like most youngsters, she'd thought these things happen to others, to older people, not to her. She was invincible after all, wasn't she?

'Smiley' prodded her lower back with the knife, urging her to move away from the door of this putrid-smelling cavern. After a few steps, he grabbed her right arm and dragged her to a corner where he pushed her hard onto an oily cloth spread out on the floor. She fell backwards, half on the cloth, half on the dirty floor littered with nails, pieces of cardboard and oil stains. Her back was hurting. Her crying intensified. He slapped her hard across the face.

"Shut up snivelling pussy. You are doing my head in with your crying and your questions. Take your skirt off, go on, and your knickers. Come on, quickly."

He was getting impatient. She fumbled to remove her skirt and underwear, still crying.

"Now lie down properly, spread your legs open and shut up. Get on with it or this knife will slice your face."

He was holding the knife close to her face with one hand. With the other he was hurriedly pulling his trousers down. He was in a state of arousal that he had never known before and he was eager to enter her. He was powerful, he had a teenage female in his grasp to do as he pleased with her. He imagined being her master, and her, his slave. This was making him dizzy with excitement and anticipation. His whole being was flooded with adrenaline. Heart thumping, his penis engorged to the point of bursting, he lowered himself on top of her, pinning her left arm alongside her body, his right elbow resting on the ground, holding the knife near her face. With all his weight resting on her, he entered her without warning, clumsily, pushing hard into her, making her scream with pain. He pumped and pumped to force his penis as far up as possible, needing to achieve a quick release. She wriggled beneath him, hoping to shake him off, but he held the knife closer to her eyes. She was crying, her heart pounding, blood rushing to her temples, the fear making her nauseous, the pain between her legs excruciating, a hot liquid sipping slowly down her thighs and to the floor. She wanted this nightmare to stop.

Suddenly she went limp and stopped fighting him, her body very still. She'd vaguely remembered reading an article in one of her mother's magazines about a woman being raped, lying still, hoping the rapist would leave her alone. She had been sick to her stomach after reading the article. She had not known what rape was until she looked it up. She recalled the big wave of guilt which had enveloped her as she had been reading the magazine behind her mother's back. She didn't know at the time that she would have to resort to using this advice one day. This was wrong and sick. She was too young, why had he picked on her? Why her? Who was he? She still didn't know how old he was, as he had kept his mask on the whole time. His voice was slightly muffled but she was sure he wasn't a man. She had no experience yet of seeing a grown man naked. But having seen one of the Sixth Form student's penis in a photo circulating on everyone's mobile at school, she guessed 'Smiley' was of similar age. She laid still.

He looked at her, his eyes blazing behind the mask. He pulled himself out of her, slapped her face and placed the knife near her groin. The longer she kept still, the less power he had over her. What excited him was to see the fear in her eyes and smell it on her. Where was the fun if she stopped fighting?

"You're messing with me, are you, bitch? You think I'm gonna stop coz you lie still. Look at you anyway, you're a mess, all dirty and crying, a complete sissy. What's the matter? Never seen a cock before? Turn around, lie on your front, slut. Do what I tell you? You hear me?"

It was easy for him to shout out insults and orders. He had learned it all from watching porn; it was his regular pastime in the evening when he visited his dad, besides smoking weed obviously. He managed to watch rough stuff on his dad's computer when he had gone to bed.

Everyone is doing it these days, what's the problem?

She was not moving, defying him, which made him angrier and angrier. She was scared but summoned up enough willpower to remain still. She felt the life-force lie stagnant in her body as if her blood had curdled and no longer nourished her heart and brain.

"Turn around, lie on your front. Get on with it. Do what I tell you or I'll turn you around myself, bitch. Stop snivelling, you're doing my head in."

He grabbed her by one arm, pulled her up and turned her roughly, her back against him. He was holding her in an arm lock. Suddenly, he kicked the back of her knees, pushing her forward towards the dirty cloth. She put her arms out to break her fall. She was almost on her knees when he shoved her forward with his foot in her back. She fell, her full weight resting on her arms. She heard a crack coming from the right one. Within seconds, her brain registered the extreme pain. A pain almost as bad as the one she'd just endured. This time though it radiated from her arm through her whole body. She cried out in utter pain. Her right arm was twisted under her body at a strange angle.

She was half naked, blood dripping between her legs, her face tearstained, sprawled out on the dirty floor. Her threshold of pain wasn't high at the best of times. Her last memory before she fainted was of the boy laughing at her and raising his hand to strike her again. Mercifully it all went black.

* * *

When she came to, the pain hit her like a boulder. Her body ached from top to toes. The lower part of her body was a painful mess. Various fluids had congealed on the inside of her thighs. She lifted her head up from the floor. How long she had laid unconscious, she didn't know. Her painful arm was underneath her. The pain brought back to her mind the memory of being shoved forward on her front. She suddenly realised what 'Smiley' had done to her while she had lost consciousness. The retching came up hard and fast and she vomited on the floor around her.

Drained, she looked around, first to her right and then to her left. She searched the darkness to see where 'Smiley' was. The noise of the trains rattling above was intermittent now. She vaguely saw a dim light in the distance, further away from where she'd fallen but she didn't see him. How big was this place? Her legs refused to carry her anywhere because of the pain and dizziness. She didn't have the energy to sit up right now either. She stared in the blackness, wondering if he was still here and if he would be coming back for more.

The silence was eerie and scary. There was no way for her to check the time as he'd taken her mobile phone from her, switching it off the minute he had met her outside the Dulwich Leisure Centre. Her mind was foggy because of the pain. She was not sure what to do anymore and whether to panic or hope.

Has he left me here? How long am I gonna stay here? What if he's hiding nearby and watching me? Maybe there's a way out to escape? There is the broken door he pulled back. I have to force myself to walk to the door, but I can't move.

She was humiliated, powerless and far away from her family. Tears welled up again despite the exhaustion. She didn't think she was able to bear more suffering at his hands.

She was a normal teenager who liked her mates, fashion, music, films, gossip and she'd never hurt anyone. She wasn't perfect but she loved her sister and her parents, even when she got irritated by them. What had possessed her to reply to this 'Smiley face' dude on Facebook? He had sounded nice and interested in her when they'd started chatting on line. He was funny and he knew a lot about films and stuff.

She had liked him. She knew now that he had lied about his age. He had lied too about being Chloe's friend and she was not sure how he'd managed to dupe her. She should have listened to the teachers when they talked about the internet and people who lied. She had fallen victim to his deviousness and had no idea when or how this nightmare was going to end.

[10]

Where the hell is this boy? It's gone nine o'clock and he is not back. Honestly he's pushing, pushing, pushing. That's the last time I let him go out two days in a row. I'm gonna put my foot down this time.

Karen was worried and angry again. Sam had gone out with a mate the night before and had come back much later than she had allowed. Today was Halloween and he was late again. Would the boy ever listen to her? He was even more challenging after he had stayed at his dad's for a few days. Many times, she wished he lived there for good and let her get on with a more peaceful life. She had had enough of his rudeness and was at her wit's end with him. He never helped around the house, his room stunk of weed, sweat and rotten food. She was dammed if she was going to clean it. She had enough work to do without that. He was a slob, a difficult and challenging child and she was struggling to like him. She loved him, she guessed. At times, it was hard to know whether she just disliked him intensely or if she didn't love him at all.

Karen had loved him the minute she had laid eyes on him. He was her little boy, and with her parents' help she would do her utmost to bring him up well. That had been the plan in her mind clouded by pregnancy hormones. She had been happy to sacrifice her education to raise the child. She was seventeen then. She left her school days behind to embrace unexpected motherhood. From the time Sam was four months old, Karen had had this weird feeling that he was watching her with evil eyes. She kept telling herself not to be stupid. How can a four-month old baby look at her with evil eyes? He was beginning to be aware of things around him and maybe that was his way to look at the world. She was still uneasy a lot of the time but did her best to ignore it.

When she returned home from work, her parents were always relieved to hand over the baby to her and not interact with him for the rest of the evening. She hated confrontation thus she never asked them if there was a problem. Sam had even caused issues at her work when she had to take him with her. He had started to grab plates and things from behind the counter and throw them, causing damage for which she took the blame. He did not respond to her telling him off either. Managing her job serving customers, while keeping an eye on Sam, was worrying and stressful. Especially when she had to catch him at the right time to stop him from causing any damage.

Karen convinced herself that there was nothing to worry about. Sam would grow out of doing mischief. She was a young mother who didn't know much about babies and raising a child. She was barely an adult herself.

She had regretted having given in to Ben and having slept with him. She regretted even more her cavalier attitude to contraception. She'd had a relaxed attitude and thought pregnancy was an accident which happened to others. She had been wrong and, as a result, she had to face up to being a mother at an age where she should be finishing her education, going out with her mates, and being interested in boys instead of staying home, feeling sleep-deprived by a crying baby.

Ben had showed up at the hospital when she had texted him that she'd given birth to a boy. Ben was over the moon to be having a son. She had no strong view on the sex of the child but what did bother her, was the amount of pain she had to go through to give birth to her baby. Christ! She had never expected such pain searing through her groin, the humiliation of wetting herself while pushing the baby out, and the hours of cramping labour pains it took to finally give birth to Sam. Her belly had been swollen and made her uncomfortable for many months. The pregnancy had not brought a glow to her complexion, as many mothers claim. Instead it had brought her a weak bladder, acne, a few more dental fillings, intense labour pains and stitches in a place she never expected to have them. Her mother had talked to her a bit about the forthcoming labour and she had gone to ante-natal classes. She was young, naïve and unprepared for the harsh reality of giving birth. At the time, she had wondered how women go on having more children after such a horrendously painful experience. The memory had quickly faded and it no longer mattered.

Even with the earlier challenges, she had loved Sam and was happy to have her boy. When he hit early adolescence, her feelings towards him started to change. With all the incidents with the cats, the self-harming, the near drowning, the weed smoking and Ben's influence on Sam, Karen was struggling to find any positive emotions towards her child. She'd heard from customers at the café, and from colleagues in her cleaning jobs, that teenage years were a tricky time for both children and parents. She was unsure whether her feelings for Sam were of the same intensity as those of other parents. She was aware that the ADHD affected his behaviour and, unless it was managed well, it made Sam disruptive, even destructive on occasions. She didn't know how to deal with it. She didn't understand properly the reasons why Sam had ADHD. She'd heard the erroneous, commonly held view that this was due to poor parenting and poor nutrition. Obviously, she blamed herself partly, but Ben most of all. When Sam had been first diagnosed, doctors had explained that it was a chronic condition mainly due to genetics, but she still wondered if she was perhaps at fault. She had been given the names of support groups for parents of children with ADHD but, as she was prone to, Karen preferred not to go deeper into the issue. She did what she was asked to do to help Sam at the time, and that was good enough for her.

These days, she put up with Sam's presence in the house but rarely enjoyed his company. To be honest it seemed reciprocated as Sam was vile to her and talked to her rudely. When not at school, he spent most of his days in his room, either recording his stupid clips for YouTube or playing video games. In the evening he'd got into the habit of going out and coming back at all hours. She had no idea where he went. She knew she ought not to have tolerated this behaviour from the beginning, but she didn't like to pull him up on things. She had been scared of him since he'd hit puberty. Why? She didn't know, but theirs was not a relaxed, close, harmonious mother and son relationship. More like strained, hostile and not enjoyable.

Is it my fault? Have I been a bad mother to Sam?

She was well aware that inside her was a place, deep down, seldom visited because it made her ashamed of herself. It was the place where she dared wonder what life would be like without the hassle and challenges Sam brought to her life. To no longer suffer daily conflicts and confrontations, to live in peace in her home, not to have to interact with Ben anymore. She yearned for harmony. She was not supposed to think that way. She berated herself for it.

I wonder if my mother felt the same way about me. What a shame I can no longer ask her. I doubt it though. My mother was the traditional type. I doubt she would have understood what I'm talking about. How many millions of girls in the world believe in the fairy tale of a mother's love being unconditional? If that's true, how come I have these negative feelings about Sam? All this fancy thinking will get you nowhere. Let it go. Leave it buried where it is and get on with your chores.

She was upset by what she'd read about the

young boy Jamie and how he had been stabbed repeatedly in various places and sexually assaulted. What kind of a sick individual can sexually assault a boy of ten, or of any gender and age for that matter? They had to be disturbed themselves. The news report had mentioned that the police didn't know if the murderer was an adolescent or a man. She struggled to believe a teenager was capable of killing a child in such a horrific way. It had to be a man surely. She wondered if the police would ever catch the killer. It was not as if they had a lot to go on from what the news report had said. But then again, the police never told the public all that they knew about a murder. She had seen the police's heart-breaking appeal for information after Jamie's body had been discovered. There was even a reward for information.

If I knew anything I'd tell the police for free to stop these poor parents' suffering. And I would gladly do it to put a killer behind bars. I can't imagine the devastation they have to face. I should count myself lucky that despite his faults, I still have a son.

She heard the front door open abruptly then slam and Sam's heavy footsteps climbing the stairs two at a time.

"Sam, get down here. Where have you been? You're late. Again. Get down here now!"

Her requests were ignored. She hesitated but this

time decided to get Sam out of his room and ask him where he'd been. The door was shut but she walked in. Sam was half undressed, his dirty t-shirt and hoodie on the floor and he was about to remove his trousers.

"Get out, get out of my room. What the fuck do you want? Just leave me alone, will you. Out now, get out."

She was shocked by the ferocity of his shouting. He was like a feral teenager, his facial expression one of intense anger. His clothes smelled of damp and he was clearly agitated. He slammed his bedroom door shut behind her.

Where the hell was he all night? What's wrong with this boy? I can't handle his moods and outbursts anymore. He's gonna have to go and live with this dad. I'm done with him.

She called out to him through the closed door.

"Sam, I'm calling your dad to come and fetch you. You can spend time with him. I have had it with you. Pack a bag with your stuff, I'm phoning him now to pick you up. You hear me, you evil child?"

She wasn't sure what possessed her to call him "an evil child." She'd just blurted it out from sheer frustration and anger. He opened the door instantly and looked at her with such hatred that she recoiled from him. She retreated on the landing as fast as he was advancing towards her, now only wearing bloody underwear. He looked menacing. She flinched. She had never felt so scared in her life. Was this her child? She reached the top of the stairs. She looked imploringly at Sam who was still advancing towards her.

"Shut your ugly face or I'll push you down the stairs. Who the fuck are you to call me an evil child? What do you know? You think you're the best mother in the world, do you? You're a fucking joke of a mother. I don't love you. You women are all disgusting. You are all sluts. Get out of my sight before I turn evil on you. You don't need to call my dad, I'm packing and going to his place. "

Such violence and hatred were making her sick to her stomach. She was terrified of him, terrified he would harm her without batting an eyelid and she had no idea what she had done to deserve this. In the recess of her mind she noted the bloody underwear he wore and wondered if he had been self-harming again. He had obviously been getting changed when she had walked into his room. She was shaking from head to toe, and her mind was hazy with fear. She would concentrate on the self-harming and the underwear issue another time.

She hurried down the stairs and locked herself in the kitchen. If he was going to Ben's that was great, it was a solution for now. The adrenaline that had flooded her body during this frightening exchange left her drained now and she made herself a cup of tea. She sat down heavily on a chair at the table. She was shaken up by the turn of events.

I can't believe what just happened. The way he talked to me. What shall I do? Report him for threatening me? To whom? Who will be interested in a teenager bullying his mother? That's what kids do these days, isn't it? He's my flesh and blood though. Then, all the more reason for him not to treat me that way.

She was utterly and completely lost. Suddenly she felt all the tears of frustration flood her heart, her body and her eyes. She collapsed her head in her hands, on the kitchen table, and cried like a wounded animal who had lost its young.

Sam passed the closed kitchen door as his mother wailed. He hesitated, for the briefest of moments, as to whether to go in and hold her, or to just leave right now. His anger won over his fleeting compassion. He flung his bag over his shoulder, slammed the door after him and headed for his father's flat, his heart a mixture of pain, sadness and anger.

* * *

It took ages for the crying to stop. Karen had never in her life cried with such depth of emotion and despair. It was a strange and draining experience. A small part of her consciousness registered the fact that Sam had gone. That, for a few days at least, she had the house to herself to regain her peace and equilibrium. She was glad he had gone. His face had been scary. She had been sure he was going to push her down the stairs. Was it possible for a child to be hateful enough towards a parent to want to kill him or her? And could that same child, fuelled by hatred, kill a stranger?

[11]

At East Dulwich Police Station, the incident room was a hive of activity. Lisa's case had been given to Detective Chief Inspector Caroline Marshall (DCI), the Senior Investigating Officer (SIO) for the 'missing person' team. An experienced inspector, Marshall devoted her life to her career. She was a curvy woman in her late thirties, who could be described as having interesting features; small but vivacious green eyes, a fetching auburn bob framing an oval face and a smile which prompted a smile back. She was as tough as she needed to be in a highly responsible and demanding position. Despite that, she had an aura of kindness about her. She was well-liked and respected by her colleagues. She had shown compassion and caring for her team, and for victims on many occasions. Having lost her first love in tragic circumstances, she had chosen to remain unattached and to focus on her work.

Marshall was briefing her team on the latest case: the abduction of a fourteen-year-old girl the previous night. Earlier in the morning, she had herself been briefed by one of her sergeants, on the content of the statement collected from the best friend, Chloe Buckley. They had also got a statement from the distraught parents of the abductee. Until the police had contacted them, they had been unaware that their daughter had been kidnaped. A Family Liaison Officer (FLO) had been sent to stay with the parents and assist them at this traumatic and distressing time. The FLO would report directly to the SIO if the child was to suddenly come home of her own volition.

Marshall was aware that the patrol car scouring the area shortly after the incident had not turned up anything. Not surprising. The abductor was unlikely to wait for the police to pick him up. She had seen a report on the footage obtained by the CCTV camera at the Dulwich Leisure Centre. Unfortunately, it showed Lisa waiting, but no sign of her with the abductor after they left together. Footage from cameras in the surrounding area, were being reviewed and Marshall hoped it would provide a clue to be getting on with soon. To avoid this case becoming a homicide, they had to come up with tangible evidence quickly. They had to find clues as to the abductor's identity and where he may have taken the victim. The girl's personal computer had been looked at by the technicians who ascertained she had been corresponding on Facebook with a user called 'Smiley face'. The trail of conversations indicated that he pretended to be, or was, a boy of fourteen, a friend of her mate Chloe Buckley. He had wanted to go "trick or treating" that night. The meeting time and place matched the information given by Chloe in her statement.

It was frustrating to her that the computer's IP address (i.e. the specific identity of the user) had not turned up a precise location and the Information Technology team was working on narrowing the area identified by the internet provider. It merely stated South London. She had contacted Andrew Gates, the Detective Chief Inspector at Peckham Police Station, in charge of the investigation of Jamie Wilson's murder a few weeks back, to see what the IP address had turned up. She was aware that there were some similarities between both cases. The location of 'Scream face' had not yet been determined. This was likely to be the same here. In the twenty-first century, with such advanced technology, it was incredible to her that, if someone used Facebook on their phone to chat, the IP address was not pinpointed accurately. Having no name or residential address slowed down the investigation.

Despite being almost lunchtime, the team had assembled in the room and was waiting for the briefing to start.

"Good morning all. Sorry to delay your lunch break. This is our missing teenager, Lisa Palmer, fourteen years old. She'd agreed via Facebook to meet a male, likely older than her, to go trick or treating for Halloween yesterday night. At the same time, she had arranged to meet her friend Chloe, also fourteen, at 6 pm outside the Dulwich Leisure Centre. Chloe reported the abduction. She told us she had no idea Lisa had asked a boy to join them. Due to heavy traffic, Chloe's bus was delayed and she arrived late at the meeting point. It was 6.20 pm when she reached the leisure centre and saw Lisa walking quite a way from the leisure centre with a male wearing a 'Smiley mask'. In case some of you don't know what it looks like, here is a picture. It has been used in a horror film called 'Smiley'. In the film, the serial killer has carved a smiley face, the emoji used in texting, on his own face. Our guy yesterday obviously wore a replica mask, sold in various shops at this time of year for Halloween.

There were quite a few people out at that time,

but no one has reported hearing anyone scream or seen anything out of the ordinary. Clearly the perpetrator's timing is perfect. He was unlikely to appear conspicuous wearing a mask on Halloween night. Chloe, our only witness, stated that he was holding Lisa tight by the waist possibly threatening her with a weapon. Maybe a gun or a knife. We are working on the assumption the abductor is armed and that Lisa went with him under duress. Any questions?"

"Ma'am, are we assuming that this case is linked to the murder of Jamie Wilson?"

"Yes, Richard there are a few similarities. The Facebook group, the mask, both victims being minors, but we don't have concrete evidence yet to link them. What both cases highlight though is that kids, and people in general, need to be more careful who they chat to. It seems that awareness campaigns on the dangers of the internet at schools don't hit the target. Kids still get taken in by liars and there are a lot of dangerous people out there. Both victims had been chatting to a person online, through social media, who may turn out to be different from what we expect.

For the moment, we have no forensic evidence from the scene of the abduction, only a witness statement. We have CCTV footage from the leisure centre showing the victim waiting but the pair has not been picked up leaving the centre or by other cameras. We are treating this incident as a priority. We have spoken to Lisa's parents and it's quite out of character for her to have arranged to meet somebody without her parents' knowledge. Lisa hasn't come home since she left for her meeting with Chloe. She didn't take any clothes with her or anything else to indicate that she was planning on running away. We have been unable to trace her mobile as it's been switched off since last night. The officers who interviewed both Chloe and Lisa's parents are convinced that the allegation is genuine, and as such it is now classified as an abduction."

"What line of enquiry are we pursuing, Ma'am? As we don't have any clue as to their whereabouts after leaving the leisure centre, what is our next move and are we going public on this?"

"Good question, Natalie. I have been speaking to my counterpart in Peckham who is in charge of Jamie's murder. Hopefully we are not looking at a homicide here but, as you all know, speed of action is crucial. We have little to go on and we need to find Lisa Palmer ASAP. Since this morning, officers are conducting house to house enquiries in case any of the residents around the leisure centre have seen anything. And, we are talking to shopkeepers in case they saw the pair. There were a lot of people out last night, kids and parents trick or treating, who may have noticed the guy with the mask and the girl. Hopefully, that might bring a clue to start this investigation. In the meantime, Detective Chief Inspector Gates mentioned that they used a psychic medium to trace Jamie's body as their investigation was at a standstill. I know ours is just starting but we need a lead to go on to find her before any harm is done. Therefore, unless anyone has any other brilliant ideas, I will contact Amanda King today."

Marshall paused to take a sip of her lukewarm coffee, while gauging her team's response to her announcement.

"She may be able to give us a clue or to give us a description of the abductor. I know she located Jamie's body, but it was impossible for her to identify the killer as he wore a mask. Even if all she can do is locate Lisa, that would be a major step and we can then take it from there. At the moment we are not going public with the abduction, first because the community is already on edge and we aren't sure yet if the two incidents are connected. Secondly, I want to see what clues we can get from the psychic before we make an appeal to the public and release Lisa's picture. I understand that she can sense people in danger. At this point, I think it's worth a shot. Everyone on board with this?"

A majority of team members nodded in agreement, but a few sceptic grunts were uttered. The SIO ignored them and went back to her office to make the call to Amanda. Andrew Gates had provided her with the number. She hoped that this was the right way forward for the investigation. Psychic mediums working with the police here in the UK, and in the USA had always fascinated her. She was a firm believer that certain people had an ability to see beyond the 'terrestrial' reality.

"Hello? May I speak to Amanda King please?"

"Speaking."

"Good afternoon. Ms King, my name is Detective Chief Inspector Caroline Marshall. I am the Senior Investigating Officer for missing persons at Dulwich Police station. Andrew Gates gave me your number as you helped him and his team with a case recently."

"That's right, I assisted in the Jamie Wilson's case. How can I help you? Has there been another murder?"

"No. Not yet anyway. I was wondering if you would be able to help us. This request is confidential as the information has not been put in the public domain yet, but we have a fourteen-year-old female,

Lisa Palmer, missing since last night. She was seen walking close to a male wearing a mask..."

"Oh God! Was it a 'Scream mask'?" Horror had crept into Amanda's voice.

"No, a witness told us it is a 'Smiley mask' from the horror movie a few years back. We suspect he was threatening her with a weapon, maybe a knife, as he was holding her by the waist. They walked away from a friend she was supposed to meet and has not been seen since 6.20 pm last night. We have no forensics, just CCTV footage of the girl waiting outside the leisure centre but not of the pair of them. The victim's mobile phone has been switched off. In short, not much to go on as yet. We don't know if we are looking for a boy or a man, where he has taken her or what he may or may not have done with her thus far. We know they chatted on the internet via Facebook and he told her he was fourteen years old like her. That might not be true, as we all know. What is the likelihood that you can get us a clue of any kind to find Lisa? Do you have any free time today?"

"Give me half an hour and I'll drive to you. I need to organise for my mother to be on stand-by to pick up my daughter from school in case I am delayed. Did Andrew Gates explain to you how I work and what I need?"

"He mentioned you need objects and a picture of

the victim. We have a recent picture here, and I have sent an officer to her home to collect a couple of her belongings. Anything else you need, Ms King?"

"No, just a quiet room for me to sit in. If she has passed already I will connect to her spirit, but if she is still alive, which I hope, I might get visions of where she is being held. I'll see you shortly. Please remind me what road the police station is on?"

"I am based at the East Dulwich Police Station on Lordship Lane. Thank you for coming in quickly. I will ensure my officers are aware of your visit, this way you won't be kept waiting. Just ask for me at the front desk. See you later."

"Great, see you within the hour."

Amanda briefly explained the reason for the call to Reine who agreed to pick up Kelly from school if need be. Reine had arrived at Amanda's a few days ago. She was enjoying the company of her daughter and her granddaughter. It was a rare treat to have them both to herself. She sensed that the split from Nathan had hit them both hard. She hadn't seen Nathan herself yet, but suspected that he too was suffering. From what Amanda just told her, it was possible that she would need her help not just with Kelly but as a psychic medium too. Already since hearing about the abduction, Reine was getting bad vibes and her instinct told her the girl was in serious danger. She would talk to Amanda about it later when she got home from the police station. Between them they should be able to find the girl. For now she had the feeling she was still alive but in a great deal of pain.

Upon her arrival at East Dulwich Police Station, and after being introduced to DCI Marshall, Amanda was shown to a small room. Amanda was sensing the same as Reine. She had not connected with Lisa's spirit which told her the girl had not passed. That was good news. But she suspected a kind of trauma had been inflicted on her. She had looked at the picture and shuddered. This was her symbol for intense pain. The intensity of the shudder was a clear indication for her of the level of pain of the victim she had connected with. Next she asked her guide for clues as to the location where Lisa had been taken. She briefly saw a black damaged door under an archway. Then several train tracks. It looked like the approaches to London Bridge station, a station she had travelled to many times. There were lots of old properties under the railway arches and tracks in that area. Too many of them. And on which side of the tracks? Checking them all would be a mammoth task and too time consuming. She knew that Lisa didn't have that much time to wait to be rescued. She picked up on the fear in Lisa's heart and soul. She caught a glimpse of an object glinting, a knife held near the girl. The person holding the knife had a mask on, just as she'd been told. She saw the abductor leave Lisa, unconscious on the floor then it went blank. She knew with certainty that Lisa had been badly hurt, quite possibly raped too. She felt the assailant would be coming back for more.

Amanda was nauseous, sweaty and her body was aching, as if she had a temperature. Those were not good signs. She had been quite affected by what she had perceived and was definitely sensing the pain in Lisa's battered body. She rushed to the SIO's office.

"Lisa is alive for now. She is held in a location under a railway arch in the approaches to London Bridge station. I know there are lots of them on both sides of the tracks, but I can't tell you more precisely where. There is a black damaged door. It is dark inside where she is, I think her assailant has a knife and that he has raped her. He has left the premises for now, but I think he is coming back for more. She is in terrible pain and may need an ambulance. I am not sure why, but I have an intense pain in my right arm."

"Okay. Let me inform my team and despatch officers to all the railway arches from East Dulwich to London Bridge and on the other side too. It is a major operation and we may not get to her on time if we can't find her exact location. Any chance you can give us more information?"

"My mother is also an experienced psychic medium. She is staying with me at the moment. If I can take the picture to her, she may be able to gather different information than me. If she does, I will call you. Is that alright?"

"That'll be useful thanks. And thank you too for the information you have provided. We have to get to her urgently and I am aware that we have an enormous task ahead of us finding the right railway arch. Please call me the minute you have further news for us."

"Will do. Speak soon."

After leaving the police station, Amanda rushed home to find her mother ready to go and pick up Kelly from school. She explained to Reine what she had seen and showed her the picture.

"Mum, the girl is alive, but she is hurt. I think she's been raped and the assailant is coming back. I've seen a place under a railway arch but there are a lot of them to check between Dulwich and London Bridge. The police might not get to her in time. Do you think you might be able to get more information and a more precise location?"

"You go to collect Kelly and I'll do my best. Okay?"

"Great, thanks Mum. I'll be back as quickly as I can. Let's hope you can get closer to the victim than I was."

Sitting in the kitchen, Reine looked at the picture of Lisa. Like Amanda had experienced a short while ago, she felt a tremendous pain coursing through her body. She heard kids playing near a dark place. She could hear trains but there were only a couple of tracks from what she made out. She concentrated further and heard traffic noise too and the name Queen came to her. The minute Amanda came back home with Kelly, Reine informed her of what she had seen.

"Amanda, ring the detective and tell her what you saw is near a place that has Queen in its name, near a park or a recreation area for kids, where the train line is only two tracks wide and it is accessible straight from the road. Hurry, he is coming back."

After the call Amanda made to DCI Marshall, it took a team of fifteen officers to scour the roads of Queen's Road Peckham to find a park opposite a workshop under a railway arch with two train tracks just above. The door was indeed accessible from the road just as Reine and Amanda had indicated. At 6.30 pm that day, just over twenty-four hours after she had disappeared, police officers found a young female lying on a filthy floor, clearly exhausted and in pain. An ambulance had quickly arrived at the scene and medics were attending to her.

* * *

Hidden behind a tree across the road, 'Smiley' watched with gritted teeth and hatred in his heart as his victim was carried on a stretcher to the waiting ambulance. Looking at the pictures he had taken of Lisa had kept him going until he would return to the workshop. The anticipation of turning a particular fantasy into a reality had given him a hard-on, on and off all day, and now someone had spoilt his fun.

What the fuck?? How did these bastard coppers find her that quickly? I've been dreaming about carving her stupid baby face into a smiley face for weeks. Fuck! Fuck! Fuck!

Sheer rage rose like bile in his throat and he swore that whoever had spoilt his fun would pay for it.

[12]

DCI Marshall had personally accompanied the officer in charge to inform Mr and Mrs Palmer of the latest development in Lisa's disappearance. She was both relieved to tell Lisa's parents that she had been found alive, and sad to inform them that she had been sexually assaulted and needed urgent medical attention. A police car was waiting to take Lisa's mother to Kings College hospital, where her daughter was being attended to by doctors. A female police officer had been assigned to stay with Lisa until her parents arrived. Because of the terrible ordeal endured by Lisa, it was vital to quickly reunite the traumatised victim with her mother.

Mr Palmer said he would make his way to the hospital in a while. He was in shock and still processing what he'd heard. His older daughter,

Aimee was sitting with him equally shocked and distraught. The sister had not been able to shed any further light as to the possible identity of 'Smiley face'. She had not been aware that Lisa had chatted with him on Facebook. At sixteen, Aimee no longer interacted that much with her younger sibling, judging her babyish. She had her own friends and her own interests. But right now she was heartbroken for Lisa, and eager to get to the hospital with her dad.

Marshall knew from years of experience that the psychological, social and emotional damage caused to Lisa would take a long time to heal, if ever. For many women, such violation was a lifetime sentence and they never came to terms with what happened to them. A lot of Lisa's future recovery rested on the support from her friends and family, as well as professional support, but more importantly, whether the offender was found and sentenced, giving the victim a sense of justice and closure. Marshall had witnessed many times that rape victims whose assailant had been caught and jailed, did better than those whose assailant was never identified or brought to justice. It made a lot of sense to her and, as a female police officer, she wished that all rapists were brought to justice. Not always feasible sadly, as evidenced by the numerous cold cases, but this was what she was striving for in her career as a Chief Inspector.

At the hospital, Lisa had given a short initial statement about her ordeal. Afterwards, DNA evidence had been taken from her body by the forensic team before she was handed over to doctors to reset her arm and assess the physical damage. A child psychologist, specialising in rape victims, was ready to talk to her once the physical wounds had been attended to. The samples had been sent to the forensic science laboratory. Thanks to a new method developed in the United States recently, instead of the normal two hours needed to get DNA results, these were now available in under one hour for urgent cases. Marshall was well aware that most DNA results were not available to an investigation team for at least 24 to 72 hours, and in some cases, even longer if it was given low priority. It didn't help that due to the budget cuts everywhere, the forensic science laboratories were overworked and overburdened. A sample could stay in the lab for months before being processed and she was thankful that this wouldn't be the case for Lisa's sample. If the offender was in the database they would have a match fairly quickly. That is, if the offender had been previously caught. If not, they had no more to go on with than before getting the DNA results. Her job was frustrating a lot of the time, but when a breakthrough happened in an especially harrowing case, like those involving minors, Marshall remembered why she had chosen to do this job all those years ago.

She had returned to her office and asked for an update from the Officer in the Case (OIC) who led the investigation team. Everyone was working hard to come up with any clue. A couple of officers were still sifting through CCTV footage to find traces of the couple, hoping to discover where they had walked, and if they were lucky, to get a closer look at the assailant. There was no progress on the location of the IP address for 'Smiley face'.

Officers had been gathering information on the property where Lisa had been found. It belonged to Southern Railway and was no longer used to store equipment to repair the rails. The door had been secured many times by the owner but was regularly vandalised by homeless people who used the abandoned space to stay dry. A police report confirmed that the last time squatters had been turfed out of the workshop was a month ago. The door had been secured at the time, but had obviously been vandalised since. During her initial interview at the hospital, Lisa had testified to the police that the door had been partly opened and hanging when she had entered the railway arch with 'Smiley face'. As it was no longer used, no CCTV cameras had been in operation. Forensic evidence had been recovered at the scene; fingerprints on the door, pubic hair on the dirty cloth but, given the number of people using this place, it was almost impossible to distinguish which of the numerous fingerprints belonged to the rapist. Even the pubic hair found on the dirty cloth may not belong to him. There was little to progress the investigation for now.

Not much to go on, but at least the girl is alive. Marshall sighed to herself. *It is good news but small consolation if we can't identify her assailant. What is it with these masks? Two in a short space of time? Surely, that can't bet a coincidence.*

In the last hour, a door-to-door enquiry had turned up a witness who said that she had seen a young couple go past her as she was going home. They were dressed up for Halloween, him dressed in black, wearing a horrible scary mask, and she, looking petrified. They were holding each other close, and she thought they had done a good job with their disguise. From her description, it was evident that the person she had seen was Lisa. Apart from telling the officers that her companion was a bit taller than her and slim, she was not able to tell them for sure if he was a boy or a man. Her description of what he was wearing matched what Lisa had told them about her abductor's clothes. The detectives' hunch was that it was likely to be a young man, maybe even a teenager, rather than an adult. The outfit had been chosen to blend with Halloween as the male had worn black jeans, black trainers and a black hoodie covering his hair. The woman confirmed too that the pair were walking in the direction of Peckham when she passed them, around 6.50 pm, on Halloween night. So far, she was the only eyewitness officers had been able to find.

However, the whole team knew that finding out where the black outfit came from, and who had purchased it and where, was going to be lengthy and tedious, if not impossible. One female officer recognised the style of the clothes as coming from Primark. She had bought similar trainers and hoodie for her teenage son in the last nine months. That information, although valuable, would not lead them to the assailant. These outfits were popular amongst young males and thousands were sold every month in the various Primark outlets nationwide. There was a store in Peckham which officers would visit to check if the outfit was still on sale in the store but it was impossible to trace who had bought it, especially if the purchaser had paid cash.

To top it all, Marshall was limited in any action she took as it was illegal for the name and picture of a rape victim to be released. Therefore, no appeal for information was possible in case Lisa's plight became public knowledge. And yet, a member of the public must know someone who wore such clothes and who had a similar 'Smiley mask'. It was frustrating to her and she wished there was a way to get this valuable information.

Two members of the investigation team had been looking into Lisa's computer, searching her browsing history to see which websites she had visited, in case she had chatted with other unsavoury characters online. Two officers, John Lloyd and a colleague, had been despatched to her school. The Headmaster was attending a week-long conference. They had not been able to speak to him to find out if he had any insight on a possible suspect or motive. They were advised to come back to interview the Headmaster upon his return.

They asked permission to talk to Lisa's peers in case anyone knew of an association with a male classmate. A possible relationship that Lisa's parents and sister may not be aware of. Unfortunately, they had not turned up anything. The officers had asked around to establish how popular Lisa was, in case a pupil bore a grudge against her. As rapes were seldom carried out by random strangers, they were trying to find a plausible link between Lisa and her assailant.

No-one at the school had a bad word to say about Lisa but there were a few deprecating comments about her older sister, Aimee, who was not as popular and as well-liked as Lisa. She was thought to be stand-offish and rather snobbish. Lisa was a bit dippy but nice, and liked by most pupils the officers spoke to.

Besides Chloe who was her bestie, Lisa also had a couple of best friends (BF) at school. They had confirmed that they didn't know who the assailant was. They knew that Lisa had been talking to a guy on Facebook and that she was meeting him for Halloween. They had not thought of telling their parents about this. A best mate does not grass on another BF. The teachers too had nothing but good to say about Lisa. To emphasize how much Lisa was liked, a couple of teachers had drawn a comparison with her older sister. According to them Aimee had not been the nicest student to teach, being a rather unpleasant child in lower years. She had improved a bit now that she was in the sixth form, but the memory of her disdainful attitude towards others lingered in their minds.

No useful information came from the officers' enquiry at the school. Perhaps the Headmaster, when he returned in a few days' time, would have relevant information to the case, not currently available to the teachers. Lloyd, wrote a brief note in his notebook as a reminder to be passed on to the OIC to follow up. He knew Lisa had been assigned a well-trained OIC who had a lot of experience in rape cases and who, hopefully, would identify the perpetrator and secure a conviction in time.

In a couple of days, Lloyd would be lounging with a beer by a pool side in Spain, next to his new girlfriend. He had planned a surprise holiday and, up till now, his leave had not been cancelled because of the investigation into Lisa's rape. He was hoping it would remain that way for the next couple of days at least. Too often he had had to change plans at the last minute and this time he had no intention of doing so.

For the time being though, the investigating team had no other option than to classify Lisa's case as one of the five to fifteen percent of rapes carried out by people unknown to the victim and nothing to prove the contrary had yet been brought to light. A photofit had been drawn up but, as the assailant had been masked, it was unlikely that anyone would come forward to recognise him. The investigation had drawn a blank and was likely to stagnate until new evidence was uncovered.

Upon their return to the station from the school,

the officers informed Marshall of their lack of findings. She knew, from years in this job, that when the situation appeared hopeless, often an object might trigger a new discovery or a seemingly unrelated fact might come to light, putting a whole new slant on the case.

I'm disappointed there's no progress but I'm damned if I'm going to give up on finding Lisa's assailant. I owe it to her. I've never met the girl but her case reminds me a lot of Monica. Poor Monica, she never recovered from being raped when we were at university. The bastard who assaulted her was evil, but he was never caught. I want better for Lisa. I want to find who attacked her and put him behind bars. My beloved Monica spent years struggling to go out after the assault and she never felt safe again. How hard it was for both of us, and how depressed she'd become! I still struggle with her killing herself in the end, and I won't let that happen to another young girl. I would have failed if Lisa had to live the same hell as Monica did.

The rape of her beloved girlfriend, the lack of conviction of an assailant at the time, and her subsequent suicide, had all been instrumental in Caroline's decision to join the police force once she finished university and to devote her life to finding culprits.

* * *

A few days later, Lloyd got on a flight to Ibiza with his girlfriend. He had been a detective for a few years and was proud of his job, especially when the whole team solved a case and brought a criminal to justice. He was a good cop and a young man with raging hormones, who thought this new girlfriend of his was super-hot and super cute. He wasn't too sure how such a cutie was interested in him. He was obsessed with her and relished the prospect of spending the whole week admiring and enjoying her toned, lean body, clad in a small bikini. He'd had dreams about her body for weeks, and, if he was honest with himself, he had to admit he found it hard to concentrate on his job ever since he had booked the holiday.

Before leaving for Ibiza, Lloyd handed over the statements he and his colleague had taken from Lisa's classmates and teachers. He failed to remember the note he had written about rescheduling a meeting with the Headmaster who, by now, had returned to the school. To date, no further appointment had been made with the Headmaster to question him on a potential clue as to Lisa's attacker.

The Headmaster had been told of the rape whilst

he was away. He knew of Lisa and was shaken by what had happened to her. The teachers always praised her and her school report was often a glowing one. He remembered she had a sister, Aimee, who had not been liked in the school. He had a vague memory that, before he took up his position as Headmaster, Aimee had been associated with an unpleasant incident involving a boy called Sam Turner. He had been informed that the boy had been suspended, but he could not recall all the facts. His secretary, Joyce, would know for sure. She always knew all the gossip and everything that happened in the school. He needed to ask her when she came back to work, fully recovered from the flu which had hit her a few days ago.

Joyce was a mine of information on students and teachers alike. She knew every student in the school although there were over three hundred students. He had no idea how she managed to know as much as she did, but he was certain she would recall whatever the incident with Aimee had been about.

MARCH 2017

[13]

Sam was pissed off. He'd had a rough time the whole winter. He'd been forced to go to school, where he did not fit in. He had a few mates who were reluctant learners like him. But the overwhelming feeling of being displaced was permanent. He was spending his time between his father's flat and his mother's house. He hadn't told his father how hurt he'd been when his mother had called him an evil child months ago. He'd been gutted deep, deep inside but he was not about to show his hurt to either parent. Sam had always thought of himself as tough and nothing in the world would make him admit to anybody the hurt his mother's words had caused him.

A man has his pride, doesn't he? Why show the stupid woman I was hurt? Anyway I don't care, she is a stupid nag who knows nothing. Just as well, I have my videos and my games coz life stinks right now. School ain't fun. I hate school. I want out. I ain't learning anything, so what's the point?

He might be sixteen, but Sam still acted like a petulant child most of the time. He was still prone to tantrums, rages and to disturbing the classes he attended, albeit sporadically. He had not reduced his consumption of cannabis, far from it. After school today he had met his dad and both had gone to the office of Josh Stark, his dad's supplier. They needed to get supplies for themselves, and to sell. Sam was well aware that his dad dealt in cannabis. Since a kid, he'd seen big wads of money and little plastic bags changing hands between Josh and Ben. He hadn't fully understood why the first time he saw the exchange. Pretty soon though he had grasped the fact that his father made a living by dealing drugs, amongst other things.

For now though, he struggled to deal with the mixed feelings a casual conversation between Josh and Ben had left him with. Once in Josh's office, the conversation had turned to a random topic. The men had been discussing the murder of the young boy, Jamie Wilson. People in the area were increasingly twitchy. The unsolved murder had shaken the community and was still on the minds of people. There was a lot of fear as the masked attacker was still on the loose. This fear wasn't helped by the mention of a schoolgirl gone missing in the area a few months later, abducted by another masked person. The public had been informed that she'd been found alive, but nothing further had been broadcast. Ben had read all about it in the papers at the time and was discussing Jamie's case with Josh.

"Mate, that ain't right, is it? How can anybody kidnap a young lad like that, kill him and do all kinds of things to him? What if it had been my Sam this maniac had taken? This kind of stuff turns my stomach, coz it ain't a film. It's for real and he was just a kid. That's sick and pervy. I'm glad this psychic woman found his body. Mind you I ain't into this spirit crap, but at least the body didn't stay hidden for years."

All of a sudden, Josh nodded and leant towards Ben who was standing by the side of his desk. When he spoke his voice was conspiratorial and low. He beckoned Ben to get closer.

"Here, Ben, I'm gonna tell you something. But you need to keep your trap shut alright? The medium woman. I know her. She is my sister-in-law. My brother told me the police asked her to find where Jamie was. She saw where Jamie's body was. Then, on Halloween night she saw where the kidnapped girl was and that she'd been raped. See, the TV and the papers didn't say that, did they? But you gotta keep schtum about it. Got it?"

"Bloody hell, Josh, you know her? What's her name then, the papers didn't say."

"It's Amanda King, she's the wife of my brother Nathan. A bit stuck up. Don't like her much if I'm honest. Her kid, Kelly, is like a mini her, all prim and proper like. A right pair, they are. My brother is embarrassed by what she does. I mean, fancy your woman making a living talking to the dead. That's stuff from the movies, ain't it? Not real life."

While this claim to fame seemed to give Josh a bit of kudos in Ben's eyes, Sam was mulling over what he'd just heard.

Fancy this creep Josh knowing the medium. Of all the people, it had to be him. And she has a kid. I wonder how old the kid is. Interesting.

An audible snort escaped from Sam's throat. The two men turned to him puzzled.

"What's up with you, son?"

"Nothing, dad. Just wondering how this woman does it. I mean, how does she know? How can she see bodies or people in danger? It's too weird. I'd kinda like to know more about it. "

"What d'you wanna know that for, you daft git? It's nothing but mumbo-jumbo. You gotta learn man stuff, proper stuff like where to get the best drugs, where to sell them and how to make money and that."

Not having had any ambition for his own life, Ben had not envisaged his off-spring doing anything different with his life. If drug dealing was good enough for him, then it was good enough for Sam too.

Even though Sam was listening to Ben mocking him for his interest in the psychic's abilities, his mind was elated at finding out her identity and the ease with which he might be able to locate her. All he had to do was to ask Josh a few questions about his brother, his wife and the kid, and he would know where to find this woman.

"Why do you need to know more about this weird woman?" His dad had asked him a few seconds ago.

If only he knew why. Sam briefly wondered what Ben's reaction would be if he told him the real reason. Would Ben be angry, shocked, appalled or amused? Or think his son was a cool dude? It was hard to know how Ben would react. One thing was sure though, in Sam's mind, his father's life had not been exemplary and he wasn't a good parental role-model. To Sam's knowledge, he had done many things outside the law. Being here, regularly buying drugs from Josh to sell to as many people as possible, was one of them. He suspected that he might have inherited his dad's bad genes.

He needed to know more about this Amanda King. His mind was darting from thought to thought. He had to formulate a plan to get as much information as possible. If he were able to look at Josh's mobile phone, he might find a contact number or an address. Or perhaps in the office computer. He'd taught himself how to hack into a computer months ago. All he needed to do was to come back at night to Josh's office and get the information he needed from the computer on the desk in the corner.

As the two men carried on talking, Sam was looking around to see if there were cameras or infrared devices connected to an alarm. There was one in the far corner almost facing the door but none facing the small window to the PortaKabin Josh used as his office. He checked out the brand of computer. It was a Dell. Sam was familiar with them, it would be no problem to get into it.

When the two men had concluded their business, Ben and Sam had returned home. On the way back Sam informed Ben that he might spent the next few nights at Karen's. If he said he was going there, Ben was unlikely to question him about his whereabouts in the night. It helped that his mother and father no longer communicated with each other. He had consistently used one or the other as an alibi to avoid providing them with info on his whereabouts. At times, Sam thought that neither of his parents gave a damn about him. He felt let down. These surges of vulnerability and wishful thinking always took him by surprise and made him uneasy. Usually, he was inclined to bury them deep down and not address them. He had seen his mother do the same for many years and Sam thought it was a normal way to act.

What kind of parents never questioned their kids about what they do and where they go? Parents who don't give a toss, that's what. Bloody hell, I wish one of them cared enough to find out what I'm up to. It's handy to come and go as I please but, one day, just one day, maybe one or the other might bother to ask me about my life. Stop dreaming, you silly sod. It ain't gonna happen, move on. Do what you've always done. Do what the hell you want, all by yourself...

Having chastised himself, Sam grabbed his backpack from his bedroom, put a few things in, said bye to his dad and then slammed the door behind him, supposedly on his way to his mother's.

It was too early to return to Josh's office as he needed to wait until night fell properly and the streets in the area were deserted. What was he going to do until midnight?

All the talk of the medium and the kidnapped girl

had sent his hormones in a spin. He was remembering what he'd imagined doing to Lisa. But his anger was rising in equal measure when thinking of the woman who had thwarted his plans. She would definitely have to pay for this. He was torn between these two strong emotions; lust and anger. He was undecided what to do about them both. He had these conflicting emotions regularly and didn't know how to deal with them. That's when he missed having a father to talk to about this. Normally he released his pent-up sexual frustration by watching hard-core porn. Or he played sadistic games on 'Slender Man'. This partly assuaged his thirst for violence and for hurting another person.

Tonight this wasn't an option as he had to kill a few hours outside, away from his mother's place. There was a small café where he hung around with his mates after school. It closed late, and it was okay for him to spend a couple of hours in the warm, eating fried food. Sam didn't have to worry too much about money. Needless to say the concept of him getting pocket money from either of his parents was absurd. Still, he had devised means of getting cash when he needed it. He had earned quite a bit of money selling packets of his father's cannabis to a few mates at school. If he was caught, he risked being expelled. He didn't care but he had sworn his mates to secrecy as to the source of the cannabis, just in case any of them were to get in trouble. He had a little stash of money gained from selling drugs, but he regularly stole money from Karen's purse too. The woman had never mentioned anything to him about this. Just like his dad never challenged him as to why his bags of cannabis were going down a bit too quickly.

Another example of them not giving a fuck. They can't even be bothered to ask me about my thieving. Sad gits, the pair of them.

The rare times Sam was honest with himself, he admitted that his parents' negligence and indifference upset him. He had learned over the years that his parents were what they were, never the nurturing kind. Most of the time he did not give a damn. It gave him a lot of freedom which he exploited to his advantage, going out with mates as and when he pleased, and came home at the time he fancied. Occasionally he felt a bit lost and in need of parental guidance, but that was not on offer. He simply toughened up and got on with his life. Lately it had been a bit more difficult and he had felt lost at times.

He ordered himself food in the warm café and got to thinking how to get into Josh's office without being caught. Then he needed to hack into the computer and get an address or details as to where this woman, Amanda, might be living. He had realised during his visit earlier today that the small window didn't close properly. Although it was quite small, he was confident he would fit through to let himself in. He had worked out his plan for the break-in. He had a torch in his bag, a few tools in case he needed to remove the small glass pane in the window, a pair of gloves, a black hoodie and black trainers. He had broken into a couple of abandoned places before but had never broken into an office. The thought of it was giving him a rush of adrenaline which in turn led him to feeling quite lustful. A perverse thought formed in this head; a way to entertain himself for a while and to relieve his lust at the same time. He decided to go out and see who he could find in the street. Maybe a girl on her own and take it from there. He felt excited already at the thought of the chase. He just had to be clever enough not to get caught. His ultimate goal was still to break into Josh's office tonight.

Sam had finished his food and it was time for action. He zipped up his jacket over his hoodie, flicked the hood over his head, slung his bag on his back, and made his way out of the café at around 11 pm. The March night was cold and foggy. Most convenient for Sam to carry out his plans. He knew many women walked back home from the nearby pubs and restaurants or from the station. A few were foolish enough to use the badly lit alleyway as a cut-through from the town centre. He headed in the direction of the restaurants first, to gauge the number of people who were around at this time of night. His face hidden into his collar and the hood firmly in place, he walked up the road, looking in windows of restaurants and hung around for a bit outside a couple of pubs his father had mentioned as being an ideal pulling ground. According to Ben, there were a few nice-looking female regulars in there. Even though Sam was only interested in young women, he still hovered outside the pub, avoiding looking conspicuous, when he noticed a youngster walking towards him on the other side of the road.

Sam was pretty sure it was a boy from his school, a few years below him. The youngster was small with a childlike appearance. He wore earmuffs over his short blond hair. Sam noted the sports bag, the tracksuit and the padded jacket. The kid looked like the amorphous kids in 'Slender Man'. That likeness excited him. He had obviously been training and was on the way home. Sam had caught a glimpse of the boy's face when they had got level with each other. He was probably no older than 11 years old. Both continued on their way. After a few metres, Sam stopped and pressed himself against a shop entrance. He looked back to where he had seen the boy and noticed that he was still within his sight. He was heading towards the alleyway. Sam silently crossed the road and hurried behind him, being careful not to arouse suspicion. He calculated that the kid would reach the middle of the alleyway within the next few minutes. He knew the area well. He was well aware that there was an opening in the hedge bordering the alleyway which led to a small grassed area. He knew that because he and his mates had hidden themselves in there many times. They'd often had a laugh, jumping out in front of schoolgirls on their way home and terrifying them. The teens had thought it was hilarious and it always gave Sam such a rush to see the fear on their preys' faces. He loved seeing fear. He was not sure why, and it didn't matter, he just loved it. Craved it even.

Excitement was coursing through his body at the thought of closing the gap between him and the boy ahead. Sam had brought a knife to open the window of the PortaKabin, but thought of a much better use for it right now. He took it out of his jacket pocket, held it in his right hand ready to pounce on his intended target a few metres ahead. He was walking silently, pressed against the hedges in the alleyway. If the boy turned around to check behind him, he would not see Sam. The lighting was poor, the fog acting as a veil. Only a couple of streetlights worked, the rest were regularly vandalised. He was careful to only enter the circle of light given off by a lamp post when the boy was not looking back. The boy appeared a bit apprehensive at walking in the alleyway, that late and by himself. Sam was surprised that no parent was with him at this time of night.

Where has he been and why was he walking home alone? Maybe his parents are like mine. Not giving a damn where their kid is.

Sam was pressed against the hedge when he heard a scream and a scuffle.

What the hell?

He jumped in the middle of the alleyway, only to see a man wearing a 'Scream mask' holding the young boy from behind, in an arm lock, easily pulling him into the opening just as Sam approached.

Bastard. What the fuck? This guy is wearing the mask and taking the boy. I can't believe it.

Sam hurried and caught up with the pair who were now just behind the hedge. The abductor was walking backwards, holding the petrified boy in front of him, in a tight arm lock. His right hand was silencing the boy, exposing a Rolex on his wrist. The boy was barely reaching his chest. The masked man was facing Sam, grunting and signalling with his head for him to move on. Sam's mind was flooded with excitement and fear. Maybe he was facing Jamie's killer as the guy wore the same mask. He had to find out who he was. It didn't matter about the boy anymore. He had bigger fish to fry. He wanted to know who the 'Scream mask' was.

He moved towards him, wielding his knife from side to side, showing the masked man that he was more powerful as he had a weapon. They appraised each other above the victim's head, creating an opportunity for the boy to raise his arm up and swing it downwards into the masked man's groin and hit him with all his strength. In pain, the man let go of him momentarily. The boy turned sideways and ran for his life.

Sam had to decide what to do in a split second. Was he gonna run after him or get the mask off the guy? Swiftly he pulled on the mask with his left hand. His hope of seeing his assailant's face was dashed when his forehead was hit by a hard fist. He recoiled in pain, holding his forehead with his right hand, the mask still in his left, the knife having dropped on the ground. He stumbled back a few steps. The throbbing pain in his head and eyes made him dizzy. Sam fell to the ground, winded and groggy. He had passed out.

When he came to, Sam blinked a few times to

regain focus in his swollen eyes. In the distance, he heard police sirens fast approaching. Getting up as quickly as he could, Sam picked up his knife and the mask, and legged it through the opening onto the grassed area and out onto the street on the other side. A short distance away, he stopped to pull the bag off his back and stuffed both the knife and the mask inside.

He ran away, heading in the direction of his mother's place. The kid had obviously called the cops to report the incident. For sure, no-one would be waiting on the scene to greet them. He decided that he would deal with Josh's office another time. There had been a bit too much excitement for one night. He was still finding it hard to believe he might have met Jamie's killer. He had to be smart now and decide what to do with the mask, if anything.

He had admired 'Scream face' when he'd heard what happened to Jamie. That's why he had chosen to use a mask when abducting Lisa. It'd been cool to hide behind it and do all the things he did to her, as if it wasn't him. Best feeling he had ever had. Shame the medium had spoilt his fun. She was closer to paying for it than ever before and that gave him a tremendous surge of hope that a suitable revenge would be exacted sooner or later.

* * *

A few weeks later, Josh Stark arrived at work to find the window of his office taken down. Apart from the computer being left on, there were no signs of anything being taken. Josh had locked up his cash and a tiny bit of weed in a hidden safe screwed to the floor. He kept most of his huge drug supplies in a warehouse which only one other person knew about. The robber had not been able to steal any drugs, if that had been his motive for the robbery. He was nevertheless baffled as to what the robber wanted with his computer and in particular with the list of contacts from his email account. The intruder had left the device on that particular page and he was not sure why. It all seemed amateurish to him. He was not savvy with IT and assumed that it had not been difficult to hack into it. Being a bit slack with security, he never used this office computer to enter business transactions or any financial details. Instead he used it to send a few emails, go on social media and for shady leisure activities he regularly engaged in, usually in the middle of the night. He laughed to himself. Had he been here last night, the scum thief would have had the shock of his life, coming face to face with him.

SUMMER 2017

[14]

"Mummy, push me again please. Higher, higher, please Mummy."

Kelly was in the park, enjoying the swings, experiencing the exhilaration of flying as high as possible. She loved spending time with her mother and it was always difficult to drag her away from the play area.

"This is the last push, Kelly, I told you five minutes ago that we have to go home now. Your dad is coming to pick you up in half an hour."

Kelly thought that the swing stopped too soon. With great reluctance, she jumped off it and followed her mother out of the park. She didn't want to go home. She would much rather stay here, in the warm late afternoon, and play more. She knew her mother had work to do and they had to return home now.

Besides, her dad had phoned yesterday offering to take her out for a pizza tonight. She had not seen him for a couple of weekends, therefore Amanda had agreed. Kelly was convinced her mum had said yes to prevent her from interrupting her work.

Near the exit, hidden by shrubberies, stood Sam. He had been watching them for a few days now but still had to figure out if they had a routine after school. Over the last few months, since getting Amanda's address, Sam had been conjuring up ideas on how to take revenge on Amanda. His target had to be Kelly. He hoped this would inflict maximum pain to the medium. He needed to work out if or when there might be a chance for him to abduct the child without Amanda being present. He had had plenty of opportunities to witness the closeness and bond between mother and daughter, causing a mixture of bitterness and yearning to invade his heart.

Sam had broken into Josh's office a few days later than planned. He had not quite grasped what had taken place on that strange night. Sam had gone over the events many times in his mind and still wondered if he had imagined the whole thing. Only the presence of the mask made the episode a tangible reality.

That was even better than any stalking game in

'Slender Man', bloody exciting. The fear in that boy's face, that was magic. Much more real than in the games. I can't believe that the guy managed to escape. It was cool and I was brave to tackle him. As a reward I've got the mask. Shame I didn't get his watch. Everyone is talking about this damn mask and Jamie's killer. Ha, ha, they are all shitting themselves. Now I've got it. Shame I didn't have it before, it would have spooked Lisa even more than the 'Smiley mask'. And to think this guy was on the prowl like me. How weird is this?

He was grinning at the thought of that night. He felt a kinship to the masked guy. In his mind he called him Jamie's killer. He wanted to be like him. He was undecided as to what to do with the 'Scream mask'. He had taken great delight in trying the mask on and looking at himself in the mirror. It was now hidden in his bedroom at his mother's, and hopefully she would not bother to look through his stuff. It was out of her sight in his wardrobe anyway. A few other things were hidden there, and would remain there until he took them out, almost like sports trophies, constant reminders of his achievements. It excited him to smell his bloody underwear and to touch it, knowing that the blood on it was Lisa's after he had raped her. He got so aroused every time he thought of what he'd done to her that it was becoming addictive.

On the other hand, when he looked at the 'Smiley mask' his resentment and anger towards Amanda increased over time. Before he attacked Lisa, he had watched the film 'Smiley' several times to get an inspiration on how to replicate the popular emoji onto Lisa's face. He had planned this for weeks before he abducted her, and that was the biggest kick he had wanted to get out of her. The rape had been enthralling and the memory of it still excited him. But the desire of carving Lisa's face just like in a horror movie, still bothered Sam at regular intervals. Ideally, it should have been her sister Aimee who bore the brunt of his revenge, but he thought it was more perverse to pick on Lisa.

He followed Kelly and Amanda at a safe distance and saw them enter the block of flats he was now familiar with. It had not been rocket science to find out the information on Nathan in Josh's computer.

The old git is such an idiot. Easy password, and not much security on his computer. Gosh, was that an easy job or what? Many people are stupid with computers, they don't understand the basics.

When he'd hacked into Josh's computer, Sam had unwittingly discovered a side of the man he had not expected. He wasn't quite sure how to deal with he saw, so as usual, he pretended he'd seen nothing! But, at least, he had been able to find an address for

Nathan. As it turned out, Amanda did not live with him, which Sam had not been aware of. Patiently, he had stood outside Nathan address and followed the man over several days. Finally, one Saturday, Sam had been led to Amanda's flat when Nathan went to pick up his daughter. From then on, Sam stalked Kelly and Amanda whenever he was not at school, and at weekends. He was careful to wear different clothes and to keep a safe distance to remain unnoticed.

Amanda and Kelly had returned home and were enjoying a cool glass of lemonade. Kelly went to play in her room, waiting for her dad to arrive. Amanda tackled her inbox with the never-ending list of unread emails. She was busier than ever. Having been successful in the three police cases she had been involved in, she was now in demand from other police stations. A few magazines were interested in doing an interview with her. She had more private clients too, all of them eager to connect with their loved ones. On top of that, she had to carry on training to perfect her readings and develop her intuition further.

"Never assume you know everything about your gift, there is always more to learn."

This had been Reine's way of telling her, over the years, that she had to carry on learning all her life. To never become complacent about her gift. That there was always a new deeper level to reach.

Amanda conceded that Reine was right. She had seen how her gift had become more powerful as a result of reading more and attending new psychic mediumship circles regularly. It was easier just to be a medium and connect only with the spirits of the departed. However, Amanda had been lucky to have been given the gift of seeing events ahead of time. She never underestimated the value of it. Like any other talent, she had to keep working at improving her skill. Especially in cases like Lisa's, when the victim was still alive. She was quite excited to spend five days at a residential mediumship workshop in Berkshire, in a few weeks' time. Its purpose was to help psychics develop the way they interpreted their visions more accurately, by learning new symbols from each other. It was not always easy to decipher the signs sent by spirits. Amanda knew her readings, and her psychic work with the police, would benefit greatly. She was looking for guidance as well, on how psychics can better connect with their loved ones. It was challenging for her to channel the spirits of her own departed relatives. Almost as if there was a block. It wasn't an uncommon occurrence amongst mediums. The seminar was an opportunity to learn from others how to improve on that connection.

When she had to go to work, it was far less stressful leaving Kelly with Reine than when she used to rely on Nathan to take care of their daughter. She had already asked her mother if she was free to come down during the workshop to look after Kelly.

Reine had agreed without hesitation. She missed her daughter and granddaughter as they lived quite far apart. Every time Amanda asked for help, Reine tried her best to be there for her and come down to spend time with both of them. She found Kelly endearing, a mixture of a mature "old soul" wise beyond her years, yet still the eight-year-old kid, loving to play with her dolls. With all the technology around these days, Reine was not sure if many children still played with real toys. She hoped that they still used their imagination instead of passively playing video games or spending time on their mobile phones. She was impressed how passionate Kelly was about reading. She remembered how she had loved reading to Amanda when she was young. Amanda had wisely followed in her footsteps and had given her daughter a passion for books. Reine was proud of her daughter who, in her opinion, was doing a brilliant job of raising Kelly.

Having seen mother and daughter get home, Sam made his way to his father's as he hoped to get several packets of weed from him to sell to a few of his classmates. He needed the money to execute the plan he had come up with to exact revenge on Amanda. Ben had said he was going to get supplies from Josh this evening, Sam planned to go with him. He was curious to see if Josh would mention the break-in at all. He hurried, wanting to make sure Ben didn't leave without him. When Sam got to his father's, Ben was in a foul mood, arguing on the phone, rushing out of the door. Sam just followed him, keeping his gob shut as he had learnt to do when seeing his father agitated and furious with one thing or another, or like now, with someone.

Ben raised an interrogating eyebrow when he saw Sam jumping in the car next to him. Sam just shrugged his shoulders. Ben sped off, still on the phone, prompting Sam to question how his father was able to drive that fast with only one hand on the steering wheel. It was scary yet thrilling for Sam who planned to emulate him when he eventually drove his own car. The illegality of driving while on the phone did not bother Sam. He had learnt over the years that his dad rarely complied with the law.

As they entered Josh's office, Sam stopped in his tracks. His eyes wide open were sending messages to his disbelieving brain that there, inside Josh's office, stood Nathan and Kelly.

What the fuck are they doing here of all places? I left

Kelly at home with her mother an hour ago. I don't want her to see my face in case she recognises me from the park. Oh bummer. I didn't expect this.

Sam was bricking it, unsure whether to go further in or backtrack and wait for Ben in the car. He was a split second too slow in reacting, as Josh saw them both come into the office and called out:

"Ben, man, come here and meet my brother-in-law Nathan and my niece Kelly. Her mother is the psychic we talked about. Kelly, say hello to Ben and Sam. Go on. Show some manners, girl."

Kelly blushed and cringed when chided by her uncle. She had disliked the boy and the man on sight. No logical reason why came to her mind. Her child's intuition told her they were trouble. She was already upset with Nathan for bringing her here. He had promised her mum that he would never take her to his place of work again, but today Nathan had insisted that he had to pick up an urgent packet from Josh. He had invited her to go and eat a pizza but instead she found herself with him here. Nathan had suggested she could stay alone in his flat while he picked up a letter from Josh, then they would go out for pizza after. She had little choice really; either she came here with him or stayed alone at his place. Both options were scary to Kelly. She hated being here again. It reminded her of the fear she had felt the day she got lost. She was shocked too that Nathan had begged her not to tell Amanda that it had been necessary for him to bring her here today. He swore to her it was an emergency and it would never happen again. He was asking more lies from her and she didn't trust her father. It filled her with sadness to think that way about her dad.

Under her breath, Kelly uttered a reluctant hello to the newcomers, who responded back. She was tugging at her dad's hand, her eyes pleading and full of tears.

"We need to go, Daddy. Please let's go eat and go home."

"Just a minute Kelly. I need to finish my conversation with Uncle Josh. Shush now. Go and sit there."

He pointed to a dirty green office chair, by the side of a table which did not seem any cleaner or sturdier than the chair.

"As I was saying Josh, from the 28th June, I'm gonna be free to work more hours. Amanda is going away and her mother is minding Kelly for her. If you have any jobs needing doing day or night, I'm your man okay? I need the money Josh, please give me a chance to do more. Alright?"

"Alright, I'll let you know nearer the time. I'll bear you in mind. You better go before your precious princess has a fit. She don't like it here with her uncle. You got the envelope I gave you? Great, go and do what you need to do and I'll see you tomorrow."

Seeing her dad shake hands with his brother, then nod goodbye in the direction of the boy and the man, Kelly hurried to his side, eager to leave the gloomy office with the visitors. She was not keen on Uncle Josh but meeting his visitors today had proved even worse. She ran to the car in her haste to end such an uncomfortable encounter.

Securing her seatbelt, Nathan was chastising his daughter for her lack of manners.

"What is wrong with you Kelly? That was not good behaviour in there, with your uncle or with his visitors. I'm not happy with you, Kel. You may not like coming here but it's not an excuse for rudeness. I don't want to see that again, understood?"

In tears, Kelly nodded. She was relieved to be away from Josh's office, but pretty upset at being told off by her dad. She thought that he was unfair. After all, she was not supposed to be here in the first place. Was it her fault if she disliked Josh's visitors? They didn't speak properly, and they had appeared quite rude to her.

* * *

"I see what you mean about your niece being a snob, Josh. Thinks she's a princess and better than the likes of us. Didn't like us, did she, Sam? Sam? Did you hear what I said? What's up with you now, boy?" Ben glared at his son.

Sam had felt in another space and dimension during the whole surreal episode. It was unexpected, and 'out-there', that his usual down to earth attitude had deserted him. His mind was going round and round, like the blades of a windmill propelled by the wind. Despite the whirlwind, he was not coming up with a logical explanation for what he'd just experienced.

His main emotion was excitement at learning that, soon Amanda wouldn't be at home with the kid. He realised his chance for revenge was finally within his reach. It was now a possibility, and he had a week to work out how to achieve his plan for maximum impact. He was aware of the amount of preparation he needed to do before kidnapping Kelly. He needed money fast and he had to work cleverly. Sam was thrilled beyond words to have masterminded the best treasure hunt ever.

Tonight, back in his room, he needed to watch 'Slender Man' and smoke weed to calm the jumble of emotions causing havoc in his entire mind and body. Revenge was at last within his grasp …

[15]

"Have you got everything Amanda? Don't worry about us. Kelly and I will be fine together. Drive safely though."

It was a glorious early Sunday morning and Reine was seeing her daughter off. Being her usual motherly self, she was still treating her the way she had when Amanda was younger.

"Yes, mum! I'm all packed and ready to go. I have left the schedule for Kelly's school and activities on the fridge. As you know participants are not allowed phones. In case of an emergency, ring the hotel reception. But I'm sure you won't need to. Thank you for coming down to take care of Kelly. I know she is in good hands. Enjoy your time together, you two. I love you."

The two women embraced each other tightly.

Next Amanda lifted her daughter into her arms and gave her a huge hug.

"Be good munchkin. Tomorrow Grandma is taking you to school, do what she tells you. If I can, I will call you or text tonight, but it might be difficult. I trust you'll be a good girl and I'll see you in a few days. Love you to the moon and back…"

Her voice betrayed her upset at leaving her young daughter, but she was excited to attend the workshop. Nevertheless, she was happy knowing her mother, rather than Nathan, was looking after Kelly. Those two hit it off, and she knew they would have a great time over the next few days.

"Love you too, loads and loads, Mummy. I'm gonna miss you a lot." Kelly's voice was trembling as she was fighting back the tears. She didn't want to upset her mother. "See you in a few days, Mummy."

Amanda let go of her, got in her car and waved from the car window as she drove away. Her mother and her daughter waved back, blowing kisses and she felt lucky to have them in her life.

Driving up the road, she briefly noticed on the pavement, what she thought to be a man wearing a black hoodie. He was dressed in black from head to toes. He was heading in the same direction, but ahead of her.

Strange way to dress for June. He will be hot later. It's gonna be a scorcher today.

Amanda didn't usually bother observing what people wore but the sight of the man all in black at 8 am on a glorious late June morning was rather incongruous and had caught her attention.

She shrugged her shoulders and concentrated on merging with the traffic on the busy road ahead. It would take her at least two hours according to Via Michelin Route Planner. She had to get going to arrive at the venue in good time for the start at 10.30 am.

Sam, concealed by his black hoodie, was in high spirits. His mind was a mixture of elation, apprehension, excitement and his body was pumped up with adrenaline. He had not been sleeping well since hearing that Amanda was going away for a few days. His brain had gone into overdrive working out all the details of his plan.

Today the countdown started. On Day One, he had come to Amanda's flat to witness her departure and check that the kid was indeed with the grandmother. He hadn't believed his luck when he'd heard that Kelly was staying at home with her grandmother instead of going to Nathan's. That alternative would have put the kibosh on his plans for sure. Unknowingly, the psychic had made things easier for him.

He had errands to run before he abducted Kelly. He was chuffed with himself and the high level of details and creativity he'd brought to his plan. Watching horror films, thrillers and playing video games over the years had given him lots of helpful pointers. He was eager to see how his ideas were going to pan out. One thing was sure, he was planning to have fun in the process. He knew the outcome: Kelly was going to die. The in-between was a journey he had taken his first step on.

He had the urge to rub his hands together and laugh out loud with an evil laugh like the character Dastardly in Thunderbirds. Because of his evil streak, it was the only character Sam related to in all the kid's cartoons. In his opinion, the rest was soppy mush. Today a part of Sam felt dastardly and yet, deep down, a tiny voice was telling him that his plans were wrong. If he thought too deeply about what he was about to do, he felt a bit afraid.

Ah well! Nothing a bit of weed won't cure.

Over the years, Sam had got into the habit of shrugging off any unwanted, uncomfortable thoughts which might interfere with his lifestyle and now with his ultimate goal. He wondered if he was more like his mother than he cared to admit. He had realised, in the last couple of years that Karen seldom delved deep into challenging issues. He assumed that like him, she probably felt they might lead to questions she had no desire to answer.

Kelly, for her part, was in a world where bliss reigned. She'd eaten breakfast with her Grandma Reine, just after her mum had left that morning. Then she'd got dressed and they'd gone to the park. After lunch, they decided to stay indoors as it was too hot outside. She'd had great fun playing dollies with her grandmother. She was lucky that Grandma Reine was happy to play with her, pretending to have tea with her dolls. Mummy didn't always have the time as she had to work and do all the stuff like cleaning and laundry. Sharing this game with her Grandma was a treat. Reine had brought real cupcakes to the tea party, scoring major points in her granddaughter's eyes.

This is cool. Real cupcakes. Mummy wouldn't allow me to have real ones. I bet nobody has a grandma like mine. She's mega cool. I'm glad she's here with me while Mummy is away. I'll miss her but Grandma and I will have lots of fun.

By the end of the day, Kelly was missing her mum. She was unclear as to what a workshop was and what it was about, but she suspected it was to do with her mother's ability to speak to the dead. She had little interest in finding out more about it. She would just be glad when Amanda returned in a few days.

Just before bed, Reine told Kelly that she had received a text from Amanda to say she had arrived safely, had settled in room 401 and that she had attended the first day of the workshop. Amanda was also sending them both lots of love and kisses and said she was looking forward to her day tomorrow. It had pleased Kelly to hear from her mum.

The day had turned out to be stiflingly hot and, despite the windows being open, little air was circulating in the flat that night. Kelly was struggling to sleep. Eventually though, the emotions of the day caught up with her and she fell into a deep sleep. She had a comforting sense of happiness, and of all being well in her world. She was ready for the following day with Grandma Reine. She was going to school first and looked forward to going to the park late afternoon, if the weather was cooler. Or maybe they would have another tea party here.

"It's fun to play with Grandma Reine." Kelly thought before she drifted off to sleep.

At that moment, Reine also reflected on the following day's activities. She decided that she would take Kelly swimming after school. The weather forecast announced high temperatures again, and the outdoor swimming pool would be the perfect place to go to. It may be crowded but it would still be fun to go there with Kelly. As swimming tired them both, they would sleep better tomorrow night, despite the heat.

Reine was happy to spend time with Kelly. She'd wondered for a few years if she might be the only grandchild she would ever have. Her first born, Joe was living with his girlfriend half an hour away from her. No discussion about having babies had ever taken place between them and Reine. Yet, the last time she had seen Joe and Katie, the picture of a baby had popped into her mind. She had kept quiet about her vision not wanting to spoil the moment when the happy parents-to-be told her the exciting news of their pregnancy.

Maybe a boy this time. Who knows? Ooh, I am excited. I must be patient and pretend I don't know anything. If only Tony showed signs of settling down. He's such a different child to his older brother and sister. I mean, how long is he going to stay at home? He is twenty eight already and still lives with me. He spends as much time watching TV as his father used to. Both striving to do as little as possible whether at work or around the house. I'd say I raised the three kids single-handedly for the little help their father gave me.

It was a tribute to her, she thought, that both Joe

and Amanda had turned out well and she hoped that, in time, Tony would be successful in his own right too. Her sons had not inherited her gift, and she never knew if that was a blessing or not. Amanda made her happy and proud as she had made a good career out of what she had been given in life. She knew how "normal" people found it hard to comprehend what she faced on a daily basis, talking to dead spirits and having visions. Reine knew of course. People had no idea how draining and demanding being a psychic medium was. Equally, it was rewarding as spirits had guided her on many occasions.

She chuckled at the thought that her husband seemed to be more omnipresent in her life now that he had passed, than when he was alive. The irony was not lost on her. How might she explain to normal people that he guided her whenever she asked for his help?

Best keep quiet about this or people will say I'm deranged.

Despite her tiredness, the heat made sleeping a challenge. Reine needed to rest to enjoy the next day with Kelly. That child, like most children her age, had lots of energy. She chatted non-stop, and it took a lot for Reine to keep up with her. She loved her though, and she was such an easy-going child. It was a great shame that Nathan and Amanda had not been able to reconcile their differences and give that sensitive, innocent child, the secure home environment she deserved. These were trying times. Relationship breakups were rising steadily amongst couples of all ages - their heavy price often paid by the children.

I hope that her parents' separation won't taint Kelly's view of relationships. What are you talking about, silly woman? She is only a child. No point dwelling on this. Get some sleep. Tomorrow is another day.

A smile hovered on Reine's face as she finally closed her eyes and snored gently until the morning.

Miles away, in room 401 of the Berkshire Inn, Amanda also reflected on the events of the day, reviewing in her mind what a few speakers had taught the group up to this point. She'd gone to her car with her mobile phone to send a text to Reine and Kelly, and told them she was fine. She found it inconvenient not to be able to use the phone in the hotel even at night, but the organisers had been adamant. This was a spiritual retreat and for five days, the guests had to live without their usual technology. Amanda might not be the only one struggling not to have access to her mobile. A lot of people she knew heavily relied on their phones being on at all times of day or night. She didn't usually, but when away from Kelly she preferred to have her phone on. She admitted to herself that she might come across as an overprotective mother. Well, that was okay with her. Unlike some of her peers who complained regularly about the difficulty of being a mother, she found motherhood fulfilling.

I wonder what the future holds for Kelly as a young woman. What career will she choose for herself? Will she marry? Will she have children? All these questions that will be answered over the course of many years. I think this not knowing, and the anticipation of good things for our children, is what makes parenthood magical. I imagine watching my child grow up and, one by one, get an answer to all the questions I have asked myself from the moment she was born. What a wonderful thing to live for.

She fell asleep with a picture of her little daughter in her mind. She loved her so much.

* * *

Sam had difficulty sleeping. Not because of the heat like everyone else, but due to the thoughts whirling in his head. He'd worked out the perfect place to take Kelly to. It was within distance of his school. He cursed the fact he had to show up there at all. Realistically, he had to attend school to avoid arousing suspicion, at least until his plan was well under way. Due to previous truanting, any absence on his part would be picked up straight away. The good thing was that the pupils were sitting the end of year exams this coming week. It would be easier for him to slip out of school during first break. He had been encouraged by the coincidence of the medium going away at the same time as him being able to leave school unnoticed.

That's a bloody good sign. A chance to carry out my plans. But it's hardly cool to hold a person captive while having to go to school! I'd laugh if I saw that in a film. Imagine the killer saying "Hang on mate, can't kill you today, I've to go to school." Ha, ha. I wouldn't believe it. Why the hell am I even bothering about school? Maybe I'm stupid to worry about it coz once the kid is dead who knows what my life will be. Where will I be? Frankly I shouldn't worry what might happen after. It's out of my hands and I can do nothing about it. I have to kill her and that's just about all that matters.

For the umpteenth time, he checked the bag which held what he needed for the next few days. He was thankful to have come across the 'Scream mask'. That weird encounter had given him exactly the right tool for what he'd planned. The few sleeping pills stolen from his mother nestled in a pocket of the bag. He checked the basic phone he had got at a discounted rate. He had borrowed the Polaroid camera his mother kept in her wardrobe. He was sure she wouldn't miss it. Sam had not seen her use it for years. Once again he felt pleased with his ingenuity. He had got his stash of weed, a flask and plenty of water. He had taken the sharpest knife he had found at his dad's. It was a long, sharp bladed carving knife and he imagined the damage it was capable of inflicting to soft human flesh when plunged in with force.

He had decided to return to his mother's the night of the abduction. The following day, he would show up for school registration and one of the exams. Then he would have to leave the school at break and carry out a few tasks. All going well, he would not return to school that afternoon but would go back to his mother's as if nothing had happened. Karen was weak and Sam did what he wanted most of the time. He knew being questioned about his comings and goings was unlikely at Karen's. She was scared of him which gave him an edge over her. Terrorising his mother allowed him the freedom he craved to go about his life and carry out his revenge unchallenged. He had waited for months for the right opportunity. His patience had paid off, the end was in sight. He tasted victory already.

Tomorrow, Day Two of Amanda's absence, was D day for Sam.

[16]

The thousands of tiny watery darts falling on her skin, all over her body, were invigorating to Amanda. She loved nothing better than a great start of the day and this was top of her list.

Hum… There's a lot to be said for powerful showers, especially in hotel rooms. I need to get one like that at home. One day maybe.

She heard a couple of loud knocks on her door. She put a bathrobe on while walking towards it.

"Hold on, I'm coming. Hi. What is it?"

The hotel receptionist stood in front of her, rather flushed and agitated.

She blurted out: "I have a message from your mother. She rang a few minutes ago, asking us to tell you to ring her urgently. She tried your mobile on the off-chance it was switched on. She didn't give me any detail, she just asked for you to ring her. I came up straightaway to tell you. I hope it's not too serious."

Alarmed, Amanda thanked her. Gloom and foreboding squeezed her heart and guts. She stumbled back into the room as if winded by a punch in the stomach. What was going on? She rushed to switch her mobile phone on, noticing the missed call listed on the now-lit screen. With trepidation, she dialled her mother's number. At that moment, a deep awareness that life was about to change descended on her.

"Mum, it's me. What's going on? Is everything okay?"

"Amanda, she's gone, Kelly's gone… I went to wake her up but she isn't there. Her bed is empty. "

Reine sounded distraught. As she explained to Amanda what had happened, her tone of voice rose through sheer panic. Reine's calm and clear thinking had deserted her the minute she had entered Kelly's room, seen the crumpled bed clothes and the empty bed. She had rushed to the kitchen in case the little girl had already got up. Nobody. She had checked the front room. No Kelly there. She knew she would find no one in the bathroom either. Reine had gone there herself before going to Kelly's room. She'd called out her granddaughter's name. No answer. Just an overwhelming silence instead of the happy chatter between a child and her grandmother. She tried to open the front door. It was locked just as she had left it the previous night. Because of the fog in her brain and her rising panic, she forgot to check if the key was hanging in its usual place, on the hook by the door. Remembering yesterday's heat and the windows left open, she rushed back into Kelly's room. She stared at the top window. It was fully opened. They were in a first floor flat so either Kelly had left her room through the window and jumped, or an intruder had come up into her room the same way. This realisation sent her body into a series of uncontrollable shudders followed by cold sweat. Tears were wetting her face.

Oh my God! What if she has been kidnapped? And by whom? This can't be happening, I didn't hear anything. It's my fault. I should never have left the windows open. There has to be an explanation. I just can't believe it. What happened to this child? This is a nightmare, surely there is a logical explanation for this.

She had grabbed onto that thought with all her heart. The idea of Kelly having been abducted whilst she had slept through the whole episode made her feel like retching. Waves of nausea, fear and guilt overwhelmed her.

Get yourself together. You need to regain your senses.

You are imagining the worse but think. Maybe there is a plausible explanation. Stop being alarmist and pull yourself together. This is not the time to lose your mind. Be practical. Calm down a bit and get moving. Call Amanda first.

She had picked up her phone, dialled Amanda's mobile in case it was on. It had gone onto voicemail. Instead of wasting more time, Reine had dialled the number of the hotel and asked the receptionist to get Amanda to ring her mother. The minutes between the end of that call and hearing her daughter's voice had been like hours and the most scary and uncomfortable minutes she had ever lived through.

"Mum, what are you talking about, where's Kelly? You're scaring me. How can she not be at home, in her bed? Where have you looked for her? Did you call her dad in case she went to his place in the night? Although, I don't see how that's possible. Did you call the police? "

"I haven't yet. What if she'd run away and gone to Nathan without telling me? I had to check with you. She's never done that before, has she? Oh, Amanda, I'm sorry. I don't know where she is or what to think?"

"Did you hear anything during the night? Did you see anything unusual last night or when you got up? Was she upset with me leaving her yesterday morning? Mum, what if she has run away to join me in this hotel? No, that can't be. She is too young to think about this. This is crazy. Tell me this is not happening."

Amanda sought reassurance from her mother, all the while knowing deep down that a terrible thing had happened.

How did I not sense Kelly was in danger? I should have been alerted that something was wrong. Kelly and I have such a deep connection. This is strange that I failed to sense whatever she felt. My poor Kelly, where are you?

Reine interrupted her thoughts to give her the little information she had.

"Amanda, I left the window slightly open last night because of the heat. I checked the one in Kelly's room just now and it's fully open. Do you think she is able to climb out of it and jump from the first floor?"

"These windows have a red safety catch on the side of the window frame. Go and check if it's still on. Quickly Mum. If it's broken, it can't be Kelly who opened it. She wouldn't know what to do or that it's even there. Go check, please …"

"Okay, I'm looking. Yes, there is a red plastic catch. It has been lifted up. What does it mean Amanda?"

"Mum, call the police right away. It means a

person who knew what to do, forced the safety catch to open the window fully, got into her room through it and kidnapped her."

"This is absurd. How about getting out of the flat? They both risked being hurt by jumping out of the window or being seen. And Kelly would have screamed and woken me up. It doesn't make sense… "

"Have you checked the front door? Was it locked last night? Is it still locked now? Check it, please."

Amanda was getting hysterical. She had to rely on her mother for any information about Kelly, and that irritated her. She was impatient and powerless.

Reine went back to the front door she had already checked and looked for the key to unlock it. The hook was empty.

Oh my God. Whoever took Kelly went out with her through the front door, then locked the door behind them. I guess that was to stop me leaving the flat in case I heard anything.

The thought that this abduction had been carefully planned loomed in her mind.

"Amanda, the key is gone… I checked the door this morning but forgot to check the key. It's gone. I am locked in. That's how Kelly left the flat. What shall I do?"

"I'm packing and coming back straightway. Don't

touch the door or the window and call the police. Tell them Kelly has been abducted during the night and I'll get home as soon as I can. And, Mum, ring Nathan now. Tell him what's happened. Tell him to bring his key to the flat. He never gave it back. I'll ring you during the journey in case there is any news. This can't be happening."

Amanda had gone on automatic pilot, shocked and unable to cry. She knew she had to get back home and help bring her only child home safe and unharmed. Her priority was to find her daughter. Any strong emotions distracting her from that goal had to remain buried until she knew more about what had occurred last night. A glimpse of a sleepy Kelly entered her mind but nothing else. For once in her life, she was unable to see what she was desperate to see. She was too agitated to be grounded and to connect with Kelly. She thought it best to just pack and drive back to the flat as quickly as possible. The police would get to her place and start their work before she arrived. There would be time to connect with Kelly and find out who had taken her and where he/she held her. That thought reassured her a bit. The GPS, set to home, predicted a two-hour journey. Amanda knew that the long hours of labour giving birth to Kelly were nothing compared to the excruciating, long two hours it was going to take to get back home.

Reine was as impatient for Amanda to get home as her daughter was. She had rung the police to report the suspected kidnapping. She had been told that a forensic team and investigating officers would arrive shortly to take a statement from her. She'd spoken to Nathan who hadn't fared much better than Amanda at the news of his missing daughter. He had cut the conversation short and told Reine he would be with her in 10 minutes. Nathan was struggling to grasp the full meaning of what Amanda's mother had told him.

Who the hell might want to kidnap Kelly? And why? Why choose her? My sweet girl. Amanda must be in a terrible state. I can't get my head around what's happened. What kind of sicko would take my daughter from her bed, in her home? What do they want with her?

Nathan's mind was in turmoil as he got into his car, prompting more questions than answers. He did his best not to imagine the harm that a man, if indeed a man had taken Kelly, was capable of inflicting on his young daughter. Tears of angers were burning his eyes. He thumped the steering wheel so hard that the horn came to life loudly. Curious passers-by, alerted by the commotion, witnessed the sight of a man in his car, angrily thumping his steering wheel and shouting obscenities at an invisible person. Nobody had any idea what might have caused Nathan's outburst but, judging by his actions, it had to be pretty bad as the guy raged on.

* * *

Had either her mother, father or grandmother been able to feel the terror that filled Kelly's heart and mind, they would have been even more frightened and distraught. Kelly had woken up startled, struggling to breathe, a hand placed firmly on her mouth. Her bedroom had been dark, but despite the faint beam of a torch, she had not seen whose hand was gagging her. She'd heard a male voice whispering for her to be quiet and felt a sharp pain in her neck. Whoever it was, he was holding a sharp object to her throat. She was petrified. Her whole body wanted to scream with sheer terror, not understanding what was happening to her. She was more frightened than the time she had got lost with her dad. Where was Grandma Reine? Why did she not come to save her? Who was that man and how had he got into her bedroom? In a tiny part of her memory, a thought arose inside Kelly's head;

I think I know this voice. Where did I hear it? I don't

like him, he gives me the creeps and I am scared. I want Mummy.

With the knife closer to her neck, Kelly flinched as Sam pulled her up to a sitting position, forcing her to drink a bitter tasting liquid. Suddenly the tension inside of her mellowed, her eyes closed by themselves and she fell into a deep sleep. She was unaware that the abductor had cut a lock of her hair, grabbed one of her teddies and had lifted her onto his shoulder.

[17]

On the drive home, Amanda had to exercise tremendous control to drive within the speed limit. She wanted to get home as fast as humanly and legally possible. She spoke to Reine half an hour after her departure from the hotel. Her mother informed her that Nathan had arrived not long after she spoke to him. He had unlocked the front door, releasing Reine from her unexpected prison and making sure the police officers were able to get into the flat. Reine had been relieved to see Nathan.

A police constable, Peter Styles, and a Family Liaison Officer (FLO) from Croydon Police Station arrived at the flat soon after Nathan. Reine told them of Amanda's impending arrival back home. The constable took a statement from her and asked

Nathan questions as to his whereabouts the previous night. Nathan wrestled with himself not to order him to get on with finding his daughter instead of asking him questions. He knew Styles was only doing his job and exploring every avenue. He bit his tongue and forced himself to remain polite and cooperative.

More colleagues arrived within half an hour to search the block of flats and to ask residents if they had seen the missing child. Reine and Nathan were asked for contact numbers of family members and friends to enable their colleagues in the incident room to contact every one of them. The quicker family and friends were eliminated from the enquiry, the quicker they could concentrate on other potential suspects. As part of the initial search, the investigation team would ring the nearby hospitals in case an injured child had been brought in.

Meanwhile, the forensic team was busy getting fingerprints and DNA evidence from Kelly's room, the front door and from the other rooms in the house. Despite the obvious possibility that Kelly had been abducted, they had to ensure that she hadn't just wandered off. They were acting quickly. When dealing with abduction cases, the first forty eight hours were crucial if the victim was going to be found alive. Assuming the abductor had come in anytime between midnight and 4 am, Kelly had already been missing between six and a half and eight and a half hours.

Reine had never had cause to wonder what resources came into play to deal with a child's abduction. Styles told her the case had been classified as an aggravated burglary, assault and abduction. It was based on the assumption that Kelly had been removed from her home presumably without her consent, or her grandmother's, and that the abductor had gained unlawful entry into the flat. Following the established procedure, the Criminal Investigation Department (CID) and the Special Enquiry Unit (SEU) had been notified and a Child Rescue Alert (CRA) had been activated.

The Detective Sergeant (DS) in charge, Oliver Moon, had arrived from Croydon a little while after his colleagues. He was a fairly new recruit to Croydon Police Station but had fifteen years' experience in the police force. He had explained to Reine and Nathan why several agencies had to be notified in cases similar to Kelly's.

For Reine, the prospect of different people helping to find Kelly was both overwhelming and reassuring. She wasn't sure how Amanda would feel with all the publicity which the CRA would generate on TV and other media. It seemed a bit alarmist to Reine. She still hoped that the child would return home soon, ending the nightmare. With the questioning, the comings and goings of the police officers and forensic team, she had not found a moment's peace to attempt to connect with Kelly to find out where, and by whom, she'd been taken.

It was only 9 am. A lot had happened since Reine had got up almost two hours ago and yet the time was suspended, wrapping her and Nathan in a capsule where the day was at a stand-still. Amanda had told her mother that she should be home around 10 am. Reine was unable to concentrate on anything, at times sobbing and, at others, sitting shell-shocked, unable to move or think. The FLO had made her a welcome cup of tea. Her world, and that of her family, had been turned upside down in the space of one night. She had no idea how to handle it or what to do about it. Kelly had to be found, that, she knew. How, where and when were the questions swirling in her mind for the last hour.

Nathan, agitated and visibly angry, had paced the front room since his arrival. Unlike Reine who thought the vast number of people helping Kelly was a good thing, Nathan yearned to go out by himself. He wanted to search the neighbourhood to find Kelly and her abductor. He thought too much time had already been wasted. But the DS had encouraged him to stay put. Though requiring superhuman powers, Nathan resolved to keep his mouth shut and let the police do their job without interfering. The hopelessness of not knowing how to help his daughter overwhelmed him. He dared not let go of his anger for fear of crumbling altogether. His anger kept him upright, and he needed it.

Moon had confirmed the abductor had entered the flat through the window and left through the front door. However, only a few fingerprints had been found, and he suspected that the prints were those of Kelly, Amanda, Nathan and Reine. They would be processed and entered in the national database. One forensic officer had taken both Nathan and Reine's fingerprints to eliminate them from those found at the scene. Then he asked Reine and Nathan for permission to remove a few of Kelly's hairs from her brush to provide them with the child's DNA.

"Is it in case her body is found?" whispered the distraught grandmother.

"It is simply a routine procedure, Ma'am. We input the DNA details on the UK Missing Persons DNA Database. It helps identify a missing person. And yes, it does help too, in the case of an unidentified body."

Reine winced at the thought of her little

granddaughter being classified as a body. Her whole being was rebelling against this morbid possibility. It didn't help that there was nothing for both Reine and Nathan to do apart from waiting for Amanda's return and the enforced wait was agonising. Anxiety was suffocating Reine, making it challenging for her to breathe inside the flat. She felt stifled by the hustle and bustle of the forensic team. She decided to sit in the communal gardens. It would be better for her if she stayed outside and calmed herself down. She might even get a vision of Kelly.

At 9.50 am, Amanda, at last, arrived home. Reine had been relieved to see her park the car and rushed to her. Mother and daughter hugged tightly. In that embrace, they shared their deepest fear and sorrow. Amanda had made it home. Feeling the adrenaline leaving her body, she allowed herself to cry. Utterly distraught, her eyes rimmed with red, Reine apologised to Amanda for Kelly's disappearance. Their shared grief weighed them down and the two women instinctively supported each other to walk back to the flat. Nathan was waiting for Amanda at the door. She rushed into his arms. She rested her face on Nathan's chest, her tears finally free to flow, wetting his shirt. He was holding her tight, whispering soothing noises in her ear. It felt good and reassuring to be held in his strong arms. Amanda almost believed all would be well.

"Ms King, I am Detective Sergeant Oliver Moon. I'm sorry about your daughter's disappearance and please be assured we're doing everything we can to find her. I need to talk to you and ask you questions. Are you up to it?"

Amanda turned around to face a tall, slightly heavyset man. He had a dishevelled look as if his suit had been worn several days in a row. Or as if he had spent hours in a car or sitting at his desk. His face was angular, long and might not appeal to everyone. However, one attribute made Oliver Moon noticeable; his piercing blue eyes, a striking contrast to his short dark hair. He reminded her of Mel Gibson a few decades ago.

"Hello, Detective Sergeant. Is there any news yet? What do you need to ask me?"

"The forensic team has taken fingerprints from the flat and Kelly's room. We need to know if anything has been taken from her room or if anything looks out of place. It might give us a clue to follow and work on. Would you please have a look?"

"Yes, of course."

Walking into the bedroom, Amanda choked up at the sight of the empty bed and the open window.

Kelly's smell was still in the room. The tears were making her surroundings look hazy. Wiping them with her hand, Amanda took a good look around. Dolly was at the top of the bed, near the pillow, which was her usual spot. The top sheet was pulled back in a crumpled-up mess.

Amanda yearned to lie on the bed, hold the sheet that had covered Kelly and fill her lungs with the smell of her beloved daughter. She felt a disturbing emptiness in the fabric of her body. Every bone, every nerve, every cell, every muscle taut, needing, and craving her flesh and blood. Her fingers were tingling from the desire to stroke everything Kelly had loved and touched. She was seeking contact with her, however minute. Her heart was aching at the sight of the room which had been Kelly's world until a few hours ago.

"Is there anything missing, or out of place Ms King?"

A window seat held Kelly's collection of bears and other furry toys. They normally sat in a nice orderly row, but a couple were half hanging from the seat, others laying on the floor, all squashed up. It dawned on Amanda that the toys had been trampled on by the intruder when he'd come in through the window above.

"We have taken fingerprints and pictures of these

toys and searched for footprints or DNA on the animals. Please leave them as they are now. They may be messed up but can you see if all of your daughter's toys are here?"

Amanda did a mental inventory of the toys. Her face was pensive. She turned around to look on the bed and in the rest of the room.

"One bear is missing. A brown bear with a straw hat and a purple dress. Kelly made it at the Bear Factory a few months ago. It's not here. "

"Okay. I will ask my colleague to put it on record. Anything else in the room which you notice is different, Ms King?"

Amanda focused her attention on the rest of the room and rested her eyes on a small desk which had given her child a lot of pleasure. As well as reading, Kelly had enjoyed drawing and writing. Nathan and Amanda had bought her a toy school desk when she was three. Kelly often pretended she was at school. Something caught Amanda's eyes.

"What's this? Under her book, there…"

"Don't touch it. Point to it!"

Moon had stepped forward quickly before Amanda had reached the desk. A corner of a white envelop was sticking out from under one of Kelly's storybooks.

"Am I right in saying you haven't seen this before

Ms King? If you don't recognise it, it may have been left by the abductor. We need to take a picture, and then we'll open it. Nick, come over here. Take a couple of pictures of the desk and the envelope please."

Nick, a SOCO officer, made his way to the bedroom and duly photographed the corner of the envelope on Kelly's desk. Moon donned gloves and pulled it fully from under the book. Amanda had no idea what it contained but was eager to find out. A sliver of hope rose in her consciousness. Maybe this was a clue about Kelly's whereabouts. The DS gave her a questioning look. She nodded that he could indeed open the envelope.

Inside was a paper napkin. Carefully pulling it out and opening the napkin, Amanda, Moon and Nick saw a lock of hair. Nick took another picture. Amanda gasped. Nathan rushed in from the lounge.

"What is it?"

He saw Amanda, shaken and white, looking at a napkin Moon was holding.

"It might be from the abductor, Mr Stark. There is a lock of hair inside, presumably Kelly's. Please can you confirm that this is your daughter's hair, Ms King?"

"Yes, it's hers. My God! "

Once the napkin had been fully opened and the

hair had been placed in an evidence bag, the napkin revealed its secret. Under the name "Maisie's Café" imprinted on the napkin, a badly hand-written message read:

"READY, STEADY, GO, MEDIUM."

[18]

'Maisie's café' was a little establishment down the road from Amanda's flat. She and Kelly had often gone there to eat an ice-cream or have tea and cakes. Occasionally they would eat breakfast at Maisie's on a Saturday or Sunday morning. It was a treat for Amanda and Kelly when work had been demanding during the week. The owner was a middle-aged woman who had bought the café for her daughter, Maisie, when she had been made redundant three years ago. They cooked and served home-made food and cakes. Kelly was well liked by both women. They regularly gave her a bit more ice-cream or a little bit more cake. They found the vivacious child entertaining. She had the knack of making them laugh when she visited. They knew how close mother and daughter were. They had met Reine several times too when she had come to visit her daughter and had interesting conversations with her about spirituality.

After pondering the meaning of the sentence on the napkin left in Kelly's room, a visit to the café had been organised quickly. Amanda didn't understand the message although the use of the word medium had been considered crucial and a lead of sorts by Moon. By now, he was well aware of who she was, and that she had helped locate the killer of a missing young boy last year.

Only time and more info will help determine how much emphasis I need to put on the use of "medium" in this note. It might turn out to be a real challenge. I can't disregard any information or any hunch. It has served me well in my whole career. I'm pretty sure we'll find out the real reason behind the abductor calling Amanda 'medium'. Beyond the obvious.

Moon and the constable made their way to Maisie's café in search of further information or a clue left by the abductor. Amanda had insisted she join the two officers as she knew the owner well, but Moon had dissuaded both Amanda and Nathan from going with him.

"Leave it with me for now, Ms King. I'll go and talk to the owner."

It only took a short walk for the two men to reach the café. They went inside.

"Good morning, Ma'am. Are you the owner?"

"I'm Maisie, the owner's daughter. How can I help?"

"I am Detective Sergeant Moon and this is my colleague, Peter Styles."

The two officers showed Maisie their credentials.

"We'd like to ask you a few questions. Has there been any message, letter or package left with yourself or anyone else in the establishment? It might be addressed either for the police's attention or for Amanda King."

The puzzled owner was taken aback by this unexpected police questioning. She shook her head indicating that nothing had been left, for anybody.

"Would you have noticed anyone, most likely a male, acting suspiciously either yesterday or this morning?"

Maisie thought hard.

"Yesterday was fairly busy on account of the weather being nice. I spent the day rushed off my feet, serving and clearing up. Right now I can't recall anything out of the ordinary. Apart from a bit of a commotion with the key to the customer's toilet. There's always somebody who asks for the key and doesn't return it. Instead of bringing it back, they pass it on to the next person wanting to use the loo. Then I lose track of where the key is. I think a bit of a queue formed yesterday. A customer took quite a while in there and others were getting annoyed. Oh, excuse me one moment."

A customer was waiting at the till.

"Table 5, was it? Right, that will be £12. 60 please, hon. Was everything alright for you?"

"The food's great, thanks, Maisie. You might want to check the toilet though. It's not flushing too well."

"Thanks. I'll check it out. Take care. See you again." She turned back towards Moon.

"Where was I? Oh yes, as I said, I couldn't check what happened. Having one toilet is a challenge. It doesn't help that people from the street think they're entitled to use it as well. Yesterday I had to search for the key for a while. Eventually, I found it on the table over there, near the milk and sugar. How it got there, I've no idea."

"Thank you. Tell me, was it flushing properly yesterday?"

"I assume so. If it didn't, I wasn't aware of it. No-one mentioned it until just now."

"We need to go and check in the toilet. Can we have the key, please?"

"No problem. It's on the hook here. What are you looking for?"

"We're not sure at this stage. Maybe an item relating to our investigation. We need to find it as soon as possible."

Moon took the key from Maisie. It didn't take long for Styles to take off the cistern lid. Inside was a small package, wrapped tightly in what seemed to be a waterproof black plastic bag. It had just been held in position against the back of the cistern, touching the lever arm. It disturbed the mechanism causing the flushing issue.

Moon dried it with hand towels. Both officers looked around closely in case there was anything else. They were assuming that the package was what they were meant to find. The plastic was heavy-duty, with gaffer tape wound tightly around it. Moon struggled to tear through it to get to what was inside. Styles offered his car keys to make a tear in the wrapper. A small box emerged from the shreds of plastic. It looked like a mobile phone box.

"Let's go. I think this is what we are after. The SOCO team is still at the flat, we'll get them to dust the package for prints just in case. They can check it for any explosive device too, just in case."

Back at the flat, the package was given the all-clear and the small box was opened in front of Amanda. Inside was a small, flip open phone. She had not seen one of those in a while. They were old-fashioned and cheap, but still in use. Intrigued, Moon took it out of the box. Amanda, Reine and Nathan were equally curious to see why a phone had been left for them.

"The abductor wants to communicate with you, Ms King. If they are planning to ask for a ransom, it makes sense to have a dedicated phone access to you. We might be looking at a burner phone. Or it might even be a burner app on the abductor's phone if the intention is to send pictures or anything else. Drugs dealers use these type of phones, with SIM cards only, to receive orders from drug addicts. They are extremely difficult to trace. Go ahead, switch it on, please."

Trembling, Amanda flipped the phone cover open, pressed the "on" switch and waited. A loud beep signalled that a message had been delivered. She clicked on it and gasping, dropped the phone on the floor.

"No, oh no. Not this. Oh no, Kelly, my poor Kelly. No."

Amanda slid to the floor, sobbing. Nathan rushed to her side while Moon grabbed the phone to see what had upset Amanda. The picture message was a selfie of a person wearing a black hoodie and sporting a Scream mask, standing next to a young girl, presumably Kelly. Her face was bruised. She was either asleep or drugged as she looked floppy.

The sight of the 'Scream mask' worn by the abductor sent shards of glass into the detective's heart. He understood Amanda's strong reaction. It had been made public that Jamie's killer had been wearing a 'Scream mask' and that he was dangerous. This picture put a different slant on the abduction and explained the use of the word "medium" on the napkin. It provided a likely motive for Kelly's abduction. From experience, Moon knew the masked person holding Kelly hostage was not a coincidence. If Kelly's abduction and Jamie's murder were connected in any way, he and his team quickly needed to find out how. He had a sense of gloom and dread. This investigation had taken a more disturbing turn than he had anticipated. Moon needed one of his colleagues to check the phone number urgently, although he didn't hold much hope of finding who was sending the picture message.

"Look there is a text message underneath the picture."

'CAN YOU SEE HER NOW?'

"It sounds like a clue to me."

Still reeling from the sight of Kelly with the masked abductor, Amanda looked at the phone

Moon handed her. Wiping her tears, she read the strange message for herself.

"What do you think that means?"

"I think we are dealing with a male. He sent the phone to get in touch with you. Maybe he is planning on sending messages at intervals. Not sure yet."

Nathan was angry.

"It looks like this fucker is playing games with us. 'Can you see her now?' What's that supposed to mean? Look at the picture, she's hurt and she looks drugged. Who knows what that fucker has in mind to do to her? We can't wait. We need to find out who and where he is. Maybe he's leading us to Kelly or maybe he's playing with us. What do you think, Detective? Is it plausible for a human being to play such a sick game with a child's life?"

"Yes, it's plausible. Unfortunately, there are a lot of sick people out there, but we are going to do everything we can to get Kelly back."

Despite the reassurance, Nathan remained doubtful.

"Tell me then, what kind of warped-minded weirdo comes up with an elaborate plan like that. I mean, killing on the spur of the moment is bad enough, but to deliberately set up a sort of treasure hunt, that's sick. Whoever the abductor is, it looks like he is leading us to Kelly by working out clues.

It's beyond sick. What the hell is he doing to my girl right this moment?"

Without notice, Nathan rushed to the bathroom. Dreadful nausea had risen at the thought of Kelly in the hands of a mentally disturbed abductor. It had come on rapidly and it had taken him by surprise. He was now drained and emotionally spent. He struggled to stay calm and not lose his mind with every passing minute. Having wiped his mouth and washed his face, he re-joined the group. He barely paid attention to what the DS said next.

"We now have a potential motive for Kelly's abduction. I have linked up with my counterpart in Peckham where Jamie Wilson was found and asked him for assistance. It's possible that the two cases are related. Although I don't understand why Kelly was chosen. The killer was not identified by you because he wore a mask. It doesn't quite all make sense yet."

Amanda nodded. She was well aware of the hopelessness of the situation. No spontaneous visions of her daughter since her abduction had come to her. That was worrying. She needed to sit quietly and connect with Kelly. She went to her bedroom, sat on the edge of the bed, praying to get close to her daughter. She breathed deeply and closed her eyes. She was holding a framed picture of Kelly which she kept on her bedside table. She caught a glimpse of an upset, scared Kelly.

Nothing useful to help Moon find her. And to think of all the times when unwanted intrusions have been distracting me. And now that I need to see where Kelly is, I get nothing. Blank screen. This lack of vision is not right.

By midday, the forensic team had left the flat. Moon planned to return to the police station in the afternoon, leaving Styles behind. Police officers were still asking residents of adjacent roads if they had seen the abductor and the missing child. They were hoping for a potential sighting, maybe by a worker coming back from a night shift who might have come across the pair. The grounds around the small complex were searched but close examination of the concrete paths revealed nothing. It didn't help that, following the spate of dry June weather, no footprints, tyre marks or any other clues were found on the dried up, brown grass. Fingerprints were taken from the down-drain pipe which was the likely access point for the abductor to make his way to the bedroom window. Although the flat was situated on the first floor, the height would not pose any problems to somebody used to exercise and fit enough to climb a few metres up.

Moon was hoping for clues to be uncovered quickly or this abduction might end up classified as murder. He was perplexed and that always made him fidgety. Nevertheless, he was attempting to reassure Amanda and Nathan.

"There's no way of knowing how far the abductor was able to walk with a young child without being noticed. He may have used a form of transport but we have found no evidence of it as yet. Let's see what my team comes up with matching the fingerprints in the database. Please trust us, we are doing everything possible to find Kelly. We want to find her safe and well, just as you do."

Although she knew that, Amanda had a strong sense of foreboding which no amount of reassurance managed to shift. Reine, Nathan and Amanda were in limbo. They were unable to settle, still astonished to find themselves in this situation. The wait for any news or development was harrowing. Too many dreadful scenarios of Kelly's abduction and subsequent ordeal were playing havoc with everyone's mind. Nobody had any idea what to do next.

Fed up with the uncertainty, Reine had gone back outside in the communal gardens for a bit. She needed to gather her thoughts. In the absence of concrete clues, maybe the spirits could guide the investigation. Before Kelly's room had been sealed off, she had taken Dolly, Kelly's favourite doll. It had been a spur of the moment gesture. She was hoping that holding an object belonging to Kelly might prove conducive to getting vital information.

She sat on a bench, holding Miss Dolly, remembering the joy they had both felt the previous day at playing tea party with the dolls and cupcakes. She felt nausea, and a bitter taste invaded her mouth, bringing her to the point of retching. Kelly had been given a strange liquid to drink. The energy from her granddaughter was extremely weak. It suggested to her that she had been drugged. Nothing else came to her.

* * *

It was 12.45 pm. Moon approached Amanda and Nathan about setting up a televised appeal at the end of the day, in case there was no news from the child by then. He estimated that Kelly had been missing for ten or twelve hours and they still had little to go on. His colleagues in the incident room were busy checking the sex offenders register to check if any paedophile was living in the vicinity.

As he was talking to Amanda, the phone, examined by the SOCO team and returned to her, caught everyone by surprise. The unmistakable alert of a text broke the anxious wait. Moon nodded to

Amanda and she flipped it open quickly. Puzzlement showed on her weary face.

Below a picture of a token for a slot machine, was this message:

"FIND THE GAME, FIND HER"

[19]

Nathan was frantic. "What the hell? Where on earth can we find a game with the picture of a token? Are we looking for a slot machine? It could be anywhere. In casinos, in arcades, maybe even by the seaside. Christ! This is just crazy. How on earth are we gonna find Kelly? Where do we look?"

He kept running his right hand through his hair as if this familiar gesture would soothe his anxiety. Amanda was dumbfounded. Reine was shrinking under the weight of the guilt which had plagued her since she'd found Kelly's bed empty. In this short time, she had lost her youthful appearance. The guilt, the wait, the upset, had all made her skin look like a flower devoid of water. She was wilting and looked like she had aged years in just a few hours.

Moon forwarded the picture and the message

from the abductor to his colleagues in the incident room. There appeared to be markings or letters on the token. The poor picture quality on basic phones meant the image was not as clear as on modern devices. The picture needed to be magnified and looked at carefully to reveal a possible clue.

As well as asking his team to check the token, Moon asked for a list of arcades or casinos within the immediate vicinity first and then further afield. He suggested they find the names of local restaurants or pubs who leased a slot machine within a five-mile radius of Crystal Palace. A list could be compiled from the operating licences granted by the Gambling Commission. This search would take a while. The likelihood of finding a specific slot machine matching the token was slim.

Everyone in the flat was filled with dread. The wait was agonising. Each passing minute increased the gloominess and uncertainty tenfold. An hour later, Moon was informed that a close and detailed examination of the token had revealed part of the name of a local arcade near Gipsy Hill. It was close by and he organised for a car to take him there with several officers. They had found the location of the arcade but how many machines would need to be checked before they found whatever the abductor had left for them? This was proving a challenging case. A race against time that Moon had not come across in his career before.

"We have a location, Ms King. I'm going there with four officers. I'll let you know what we find as soon as possible."

"Please let me come with you, I might be able to help. Please? I can't stand staying here when my child is in danger. Please let me come with you."

Amanda was aware she was begging and sounded desperate.

"I'm sorry, Ms King but it is best if you wait here. You too, Mr Stark. I'll contact Peter Styles when we find anything. Let's go."

The building identified as the entertainment arcade was not much more than a glorified hall with a dozen slot machines, a claw machine, half-filled with fluffy toys and sweets, and a booth in the middle. It smelt of damp and strong body odour. The grey walls had not seen a paintbrush for a few decades. Looking at the threadbare flooring, it was impossible to guess its original colour.

Even though it was early afternoon, a half-dozen gamblers were getting their adrenaline shots by playing the slot machines. Moon went to speak to the man perched in the booth, his badge at the ready.

"Hi. Are you the manager?"

"Yep. Who wants to know?"

"My name is DS Moon. We are working on a case involving a child abduction. We need to check all the machines in your arcade. I'd appreciate you asking people to leave whilst we conduct our search. Now, please."

"Okay. Okay. Just a minute. It ain't good for business when coppers are here. How long you gonna be and what'u gonna do to my machines?"

"My colleagues need to inspect all the machines. We have this picture of a token. There might be a message left here for us to find. Did you notice anything out of the ordinary or anyone acting suspiciously around the machines in the last two days?"

"Can't say I did. From up here, I can see all the machines and I don't recall anything special. There were a few teens in here yesterday afternoon and a couple this morning. Told 'em to leave coz, as you know, kids ain't allowed here to use the machines no more. The little rascals still find a way to get here. I know the exams have started when they show up here during the day. Apart from that nothing special happened."

Moon showed the picture of the token to the manager.

"Any idea which machine would take this?"

"This picture looks to me like it's the token for the machines on that far wall over there."

Following the directions indicated by the manager, Moon and his colleagues made their way to a wall displaying four flashing slot machines. Each one of them was being played. The gamblers, although clearly of different ages, all had a common look; a mixture of hope and desperation. The police officers dispersed the gamblers who voiced their unhappiness at being pulled off their chosen machine. Some were on a roll and swearing at the officers for interrupting what would surely be their win of the day. Like most gamblers, they were reluctant to let go of the machine they were working.

After all the money they had sunk into it, what if another punter came along and won the jackpot? They were unhappy and agitated. They stood by the side waiting for the cops to do whatever they'd come to do, anxiously waiting to be reunited with their chosen device. Moon had asked the manager to stand by with his keys, in case he needed a machine to be opened.

The officers split into two groups and looked at the first two machines thoroughly. They inspected the sides, the top and the back once the machines had been pulled forward. They ran their hands into the money dispenser at the front. Nothing! It wasn't possible to lift any of the heavy beasts to check underneath. In any case, it would have been difficult for anyone to leave a message underneath one of them without being seen by the manager or by the players. The gamblers watched the goings-on, either with interest or with incredulity, but all of them itching to be allowed to resume their toxic relationship with their beloved machines.

The four officers moved to the remaining two machines, hoping to find a clue this time. The last one in the row was pressed against a side wall. They resumed their thorough search. Feeling the sides of the last machine carefully, one of the officers felt something rough stuck to the side panel. Despite wearing a plastic glove, he recognised masking tape. It was holding a square, flat, thin object firmly onto the panel. He carefully peeled the tape off the surface and manoeuvred his finding out through the slim gap. The space was narrow and it was lucky he had slim hands. Moon made a mental note, that whoever had left this behind, had to be an adult with small hands or a young person.

Puzzled, the five men looked at the picture which had been held in place by the masking tape. It was unusual to see a Polaroid picture. They had been in vogue in the 80s. Moon remembered using them a long time ago in his youth. A fleeting, totally inappropriate thought came to his mind. He was remembering what he had used his Polaroid camera for when he was a young lad. He felt himself blush and hoped no one noticed. Through his young daughter, he was aware that the instant camera had become fashionable again in recent years.

The officer slowly peeled the tape off the back of the picture, turned it over and looked at it closely. Moon's jaws dropped. The photo was of a teddy bear. More precisely, a brown bear with a straw hat and a purple dress. It was sitting on a bare dirty floor. It looked like a neglected place. On the slim white stripe under the photo, Moon read a handwritten message.

"SPIDERMAN MEETS KELLY."

What the heck? What's Spiderman got to do with it? What does this mean? Another obscure clue?

"I don't know what this means but we need to work this out pretty sharpish."

Looking in the direction of one of his officers, he instructed him: "Darryl, you stay here and call a forensic guy to get any fingerprints from the side of the machine. Depending on what this picture means, I might need the rest of you a bit later, so you're coming back with me to Ms King's flat."

The manager was hovering, dying to see what the cops had found. Moon thanked him and instructed him not to let anyone touch the last machine. Darryl Sutton would guard it for the time being. The deprived gamblers were jumping on the spot, waiting to be allowed to indulge once again in their favourite pastime. One elderly man was very disappointed to not be allowed to stroke the nudges of his chosen device until a forensic expert had collected fingerprints from it. He took a seat further along with such a dejected look on his face that Sutton felt sorry for the poor guy. Maybe gambling was the only pleasure he had in his senior years.

In the car on the way back, Moon was turning the clue over and over in his head. The word Spiderman was ringing a bell, deep in his memory. He had heard the name of the famous character not that long ago but was unable to pinpoint where just yet. He placed a call to Styles to update him. He asked him to inform Amanda and Nathan that a picture of Kelly's bear had been found with a message referring to Spiderman. He was hoping that either Amanda or Nathan could explain the meaning of it.

Within five minutes, his mobile rang.

"Yes, Peter. Any clues? Oh. Of course, the murdered boy Jamie had a Spiderman bag. Christ, it looks like it might be the same guy. Alright, I will contact Andrew Gates at Peckham now to get the address of where Jamie was found and any other details he can give me. Listen, I want Ms King to come to that location. Please organise a car to take you both there. I will phone you the address shortly. I have a hunch the picture was taken in the guesthouse. I can't put my finger on it, but I think the abductor is probably holding Kelly there too. We're heading over there now."

The minute Styles relayed the DS's instructions to Amanda, an even stronger sense of something being extremely wrong invaded every cell of her body.

"Ms King, DS Moon is en route to the place where Jamie was found. He asked that you meet him there. He thinks Kelly may be held there. Are you up to it?"

"Yes, but what if DS Moon is right and Kelly is where Jamie was found, why take Kelly there? Is it the same person? Jamie's killer and Kelly's abductor? Whoever he is. And on the photo he sent, he is wearing the same 'Scream mask'. Oh my God, that means we might never see her again. He's going to kill her, isn't he? Oh God, Nathan, our little girl…"

Nathan just caught Amanda in time, breaking her fall as she crumbled on the floor, crying and rocking, to soothe the intense sense of dread and horror that overcame her when she recalled how Jamie had been murdered.

Nathan cradled her for a bit, and then helped her up so Amanda could do as requested by the DS. It took whatever little strength she had for Amanda to stand up.

Pre-empting Nathan's request, Styles firmly stated:

"No, not you Mr Stark. I'm sorry but I am only taking Ms King as instructed. I will keep you updated as soon as I can. We have to go. Are you okay Ms King?"

Amanda nodded and followed the officer out of the door, turning her head towards Nathan as she went past him. Her eyes showed fear and distress. Nathan wasn't sure at this moment what to think, nor whether the outcome to this whole traumatic incident would be a happy one. He put a brave face on it, without much conviction.

"Go and find our Kelly. It'll be okay."

The journey to the guest house was a silent one. Nathan's words had not had the desired effect of reassuring Amanda. Although she couldn't quite understand why Kelly would be at the guesthouse, she sensed they might be on the right track and that alarmed her. During a long twenty minutes, Amanda kept asking herself the same questions: *would Kelly be there and would she be alive?*

The same question that Styles was asking himself.

[20]

D-Day had gone according to plan and the day wasn't over yet. Sam was jubilant. When planning the abduction, he had banked on the fact that the vast majority of people did not pay attention to police warnings not to leave their front door key either on the door or nearby. He was not wrong in his assumption. It tickled Sam to find the key on a hook in the hallway. It made it almost too easy for him to carry Kelly out of the flat through her front door.

Very careless of you, medium. All the easier for me to get out.

Once outside, following a path behind a low wall, Sam had headed quickly towards the storage area for the bins. He had carried Kelly, wrapped in a blanket, on his shoulder. Behind the bin shed, he had found the bike he'd left there a short while ago. He had laid

Kelly next to his bag, all curled up in the small trailer attached to a bike belonging to Ben. He had arranged the blanket to fully cover her. Sam had only ever seen Ben drive a car, therefore finding a bike in the cellar of his flat had been unexpected but useful. All he'd had to do was to buy the trailer.

Before leaving the scene, Sam had used Kelly's hair for the next part of his plan.

A little message for the medium. If she is that clever, let's see what she'll think tomorrow. I would love to be there to see her face. I bet she won't be smug then.

An insidious little voice in Sam's head dared to question what he was doing to such a young child, simply to satisfy a boy's desire for revenge on her mother.

Piss off, leave me alone. I don't have time for these thoughts. The medium deserves every bit of what she's getting. She shouldn't have interfered with me in the first place.

Mounting the bike, his heart lighter after justifying his actions to himself, he'd pedalled in the direction of his chosen safe place.

He had spent time locating cameras along the route between Amanda's flat and the location. He had therefore designed a route which minimised him appearing on CCTV. His chosen mode of transport was a good cover. Why would anyone watching his movements guess that he was carrying a child in the trailer? Cutting through side roads and other emptier streets, he had reached his destination within half an hour.

Sam was pleased with himself. He recited his now-familiar mantra:

I am so fucking clever…

Sam had anticipated that Kelly might wake up after they reached their destination. She started to stir and whinge shortly after he had laid her down. He had prepared a flask of marijuana tea and forced her to drink it. He knew that with the dose he'd used, his victim would likely remain asleep while he went home to his mother for the few remaining hours of the night.

Mind you I'm too excited to sleep but I have to go home to get ready for school in the morning.

At first, Kelly had refused to drink and he'd hit her. He'd forced her again to swallow the tea, prompting her to vomit the pungent liquid mixed with bile all over his top.

Stupid girl, I'm covered in sick and I'll stink. Trust me, you gonna drink this tea if it fucking kills me.

Holding a knife near her face, Sam had forced the tea down her throat. This time she'd swallowed the lot but to make doubly sure she stayed silent, he'd punched her in the face. Next, he'd taken a selfie of himself wearing the 'Scream mask', posing next to her battered, sleepy face. Once he was sure she was sleeping heavily because of the drug, he'd left her bound on the floor.

I can't believe I have bloody vomit on my clothes. I have to go back home but it's gonna stink. Little bitch. I'll have to deal with this when I get back home. Let's hope the old woman doesn't wake up.

Sam had arrived back at his mother's around 3 am. He'd taken the 'Scream mask' back with him and was holding it away from his smelly clothes. He had not met anybody at that time of night, which was a relief as he would have had a job hiding the mask if he'd come across any late reveller. When he'd got to Karen's, his mother was asleep. Without making any noise, he'd washed his tee-shirt to remove the stench of vomit. The wet top joined other items hidden behind his wardrobe.

Having Ben's bike helped his project run smoothly. In the morning, Sam packed his dark clothes, Kelly's bear, the knife and the Polaroid camera in his backpack, and cycled to school on time for registration. Luckily Karen had left early for one of her jobs. He was proud of the fact he managed to behave as if nothing in his life had changed. He stuck it out at school for a couple of hours, avoiding any possibility of his absence being noticed. He didn't care about the school, but there was no point risking jeopardising his chance to avenge himself. He was elated and feeling a hundred times more powerful than his mates.

Look at them. Preening themselves in front of girls. Playing the big guys. They ain't capable of doing what I did but they think they're better than me. Tossers! If only they knew about last night and what I'm about to do today, they would shit themselves.

He was fidgety and eager to carry out the next phase of his well-thought-out revenge. The minute the bell rang for break, Sam was out of the door, making his way to where he had left his bike.

He was thinking back to the start of his journey a few days ago. Once he had formulated a plan, he had written it down then studied it for hours. He'd memorised it step by step. It looked ingenious to him. First, he had bought all the necessary items to carry out his revenge.

Then, on Day One, he had set up the first clue at Maisie's café. He knew the place as he had followed Amanda and Kelly there several times in the last few weeks. Phone one was in place ready to receive clue two.

The idea of leaving a lock of Kelly's hair inside a napkin had come to him whilst watching one of his favourite thrillers. Nothing like a personal item to remind the victim's loved ones who was in control here. The medium, the grandma and the father would have to take him seriously and understand he meant business, that he wasn't a wimp. The cops too. His sense of power was magnified. He was firmly in charge and they would dance to his tune if they wanted to find the girl. He had made the clues easy enough to start with, but he had no intention of making the rest of them too easy. They would have to work hard to get to Kelly.

Let's see how long it's gonna take them to find the hidden phone. They might think they are smarter than me but I'm more devious. In fact, I'm fucking clever. A bloody genius. If only my stupid mother could see how organised and creative I am, she might say nice things about me for once in her life. Let's see what she thinks of me when I pull this off. If the cops are intelligent enough, I'll be able to send a text to the medium whenever I want. Let's see if she'll find her precious daughter. Oh, I can't wait to see the woman's face when she gets to her. If she ever gets there.

Planning to send a picture to the hidden phone had been a brilliant idea. He had even managed to find a way for his number to be untraceable. Sam felt exhilaration and excitement rise inside when he imagined Amanda's reaction at seeing the selfie he took with Kelly. He'd made sure Kelly's face looked rough. And what about the 'Scream mask'? The medium would surely freak out at seeing it. Being able to carry out justice, as he saw it, had been a long-awaited moment. In his mind, he felt like 'Slender Man'. He was in control of a little child and the possibilities of what he could do to her were endless. It appealed to his twisted nature. He had been denied his pleasure and he was not prepared to tolerate this.

Who does this damn meddling bitch think she is anyway? She thinks she can see it all, then let her see what happens next to her precious daughter.

He was smirking, pleased with himself. He was aroused thinking of what he had already done to Kelly and what was to come. His anger at Amanda surfaced regularly but he quashed it down with the thought of his final plan for Kelly. That cheered him up every time.

He'd checked the arcade out a few days ago to get the picture of the token. He'd selected a machine on which he thought it was unlikely the picture would be found by anyone else but the cops. Next, he had to figure out how to get past the manager to stick the photo on the machine. It turned out the manager's habit of coming out almost every hour to have a fag, gave him plenty of opportunities. Sam surprised himself by the precision of his plan and by his punctuality.

Earlier today, the trickiest part had been to get to

the guesthouse and enter through an opening detected a few days ago when doing his inspection of the place. He'd found a room he could access without falling through the lifted floorboards. There, he had taken the picture of the bear and written a well-chosen message at the back of the picture. He was impressed that he remembered where the boy had been found and the detail about Jamie's Spiderman backpack. He had heard it on the news and decided to use this bit of information as bait. He longed to be in the guesthouse to experience the thrill the 'Scream mask' killer must have felt. He wanted so much to be like him.

Just before lunch, Sam had made his way to the arcade. He had to wait for a bit, but he knew it wouldn't be long before the man came out to puff on his hourly cigarette. The minute Sam saw the manager light up, he entered the building through a side door, made a beeline for the far wall, pretended to look at the machine nearest the wall and stuck the picture on its side. He had worked it all out. He'd used masking tape to secure it. He'd walked calmly out of the building. It had taken him the time of a fag burning to do all he needed.

He'd sent a message with a picture of the token. There was no possibility to check that the package had been found. Working on the assumption that the cops might not be as dim as Sam thought they were, he carried on as if the phone was now in possession of the medium.

There we go. Nice little message: "find the game, find her." The cops have to work out which arcade the token comes from, which machine and what do with it. That gives me enough time to be ready for the next stage.

As a child, he'd never gone on a treasure hunt. He was relishing his first one enormously, mainly because he was the hunt master! He banked on Amanda and the cops working out the clue on the Polaroid left in the arcade. That would lead them to the guest house, where they would hope to find Kelly. He let out a belly laugh at the thought of all of them arriving there later. He felt shivers of excitement and anticipation at what he would be doing whilst they were searching for the girl.

* * *

"Mummy? Mummy? Where are you? Mummy!"

Kelly had woken up, disorientated, her head fuzzy as if she had woken up from a heavy sleep. Her head was hurting. Her body was aching. She was lying down on a cold and smelly surface. She was not sure what it was, but she didn't like it. She saw nothing in the darkness despite a faint light in the distance. She was numb with shock.

"Where am I? It's dark here, it's scary. Mummy! Where are you?"

She suddenly remembered the man who had taken her from her bed and the liquid he had forced her to drink. She was thirsty now and her mouth felt like there was no fluid left in her body. She hadn't drunk anything for hours. Her tongue stuck to her palate and her teeth. She wasn't getting any saliva in her mouth. Tears of fear and hopelessness ran down her face. The feeling of terror was so strong that nausea rose from her empty stomach into her throat. A strange taste reached her mouth, bringing her to the brink of vomiting. She gagged. Nearly choked. Her throat and her stomach hurt from heaving and vomiting nothing. She was scared.

"I want water. I need a drink. Mummy, I need a drink. Please. Anyone here?" She was pleading, half hoping somebody, anybody, would hear her and bring her a drink. Only the echo of her voice responded to her. Her panic intensified.

"Who are you? Why am I here? Mummy please come and get me. I'm scared."

All of a sudden, she recalled the night in the kitchen when her mum had told her how she was able to see people who have died or are missing. She felt less queasy, a bit calmer even, at the thought that her mother would see where she was and come to take her home.

Her mother had told her about the video clips. It had made her laugh that night. Thinking of her mum now made her both sad and hopeful. Amanda had told her she'd found a couple of missing children. She would find her too, of course. With all her little heart, she hoped that Mummy would come soon. She would go home with her and let go of the fear making her heart ache.

[21]

"I can't see anything. Mark, check the rooms on this side. Rangi, go and check upstairs. I'll check the rest of the rooms over there."

Moon and his two officers, Mark White and Rangi Patel, were inspecting the guesthouse. They had not found anything in what seemed to have been the reception area. Next, they checked what looked like a dining room, but found nothing there either. They now had to go from room to room, hoping to find Kelly, if she was indeed in the building, or hoping to find any other clue the abductor might have left. They were moving cautiously, covering each other's backs, in case the abductor was still on site and armed.

Patel called Moon from the top of the stairs.

"Sir, over here. Come and look at this."

Standing at the entrance of the room nearest to the top of the stairs, Patel was pointing to the bed. The bedroom looked trashed. The floorboards had been lifted in places, exposing the joists underneath and making it difficult to walk around. The walls were smeared with brown stains. The mattress, resting half on the base of the bed, half on the floor, had a big tear in the middle, probably made by a knife. The stuffing of the mattress was exposed. It was dirty and heavily stained. It wasn't clear if the horrible stench of mould and urine came from the room itself or the mattress. Moon followed the officer's finger, pointing at an object lodged in the exposed stuffing. It was Kelly's bear holding a small square. It could easily have been missed, had it not been for the contrast of the dark coloured bear against the lighter colour of the inside of the mattress.

"What is this?"

"That's a bear and a picture. I noticed both but I haven't looked closely. I thought you might want to see it first."

Moon had to negotiate his way around the lifted floorboards. He approached the mattress carefully, straining his eyes to see what the black square was. He recognised another Polaroid picture, held against the purple dress of the bear. Putting on a pair of gloves, he lifted the picture and looked at it. The windows were boarded up, barely allowing small rays of light to illuminate the bedroom he was standing in. He took his mobile phone out, switched on the torch, and took a close look at the grainy, poor quality picture. He was shocked to see a girl, face down, lying partly on an oily cloth, partly on the floor. She looked unconscious and dishevelled as if she had been assaulted. He had the impression she was young. He knew this was not Kelly. Amanda had given the police a recent picture of her daughter and she did not look like the unconscious person on this picture. Turning it over, Moon saw a message on the back of the picture.

Just one word: "SPOILSPORT." Moon was baffled.

Who is this? Where is Kelly? What's this all about?

The DS was struggling to find an explanation for both picture and message. He made his way back to the hall and showed the picture to his two colleagues. They were as sceptical as their boss. He instructed them to carry on searching the rest of the rooms in case Kelly was hidden in one of them. The bear was put in an evidence bag to be examined for prints or DNA once they got back to the police station.

On a hunch, Moon went outside with the picture.

He looked around and saw the second police car in which Amanda anxiously waited to hear if Kelly had been found. He opened the car door and sat next to her. He showed her the picture and the evidence bag.

"Kelly isn't in there, Ms King. I'm sorry. All we found is this picture and her bear. Would you recognise who it is? And this message "Spoilsport." Would it mean anything to you?

Glancing at the photo, Amanda was relieved that it wasn't Kelly.

But if she isn't in the guesthouse, where is she? Why has the abductor sent us here?

Looking up at the DS's face, Amanda saw he was as baffled as she was, and had as little idea about where Kelly was as she did.

"I don't understand. Why were we sent here if Kelly isn't inside? I don't get it. Where is she? How are we gonna find her if the abductor is playing games with us? What do we do now? Surely we need to act and find her. I need to find her. I need you to find her please."

Having pinned her hope on finding Kelly alive in the guesthouse, hysteria and disappointment were getting hold of Amanda. The tone of her voice was rising. She had no idea what to do next. As hard as she tried to calm herself, panic kept coming in waves.

She attempted to think straight about the significance of the message.

Calm yourself, Amanda. Come on, breathe. Think. What could it mean? Is this about Kelly? What would she have done to be a spoilsport? No, that can't be right. What if it was about me? When did I spoil someone's fun? How?

"Any idea what that might mean, Ms King? I'm going back to Croydon police station and I'd like you to come with me, please. I need to show the picture to my colleagues in the incident room. Maybe one of them can identify the victim. I will fax it to my counterparts in Peckham and Dulwich in case they know who it is.

"I'll come with you but let me ring Nathan and my mother to let them know that Kelly isn't here."

"No problem, we'll go when you have finished. I've recalled my officers. They haven't found anything else inside. I'm sorry, Ms King."

Amanda saw genuine sadness and regret in his eyes and his compassion for her touched her deeply.

Forty minutes later, when they arrived at the police station, Moon directed Amanda to his office. As they entered, he showed her to a chair and asked her:

"Which cases have you worked on with local police stations recently? Apart from Jamie Wilson's case which I already know about? I think there might be a link between the picture and the cases you were involved with."

"Let's see. I've worked on a few cases of missing persons this year. Last year, apart from Jamie's murder, I helped out with a sexual assault case in Dulwich. The victim was called Lisa. But I can't remember her surname. Maybe, it is to do with her? She had been raped but I don't know if the perpetrator has been found yet. Is that any help, DS Moon?

"Yes, it is. I'll get one of my officers to check this out straight away. I'll show my colleagues the picture, give them the name you mentioned and get them to enter it all in the database. We'll see what information can help us make sense of the Polaroid picture and the message. Thanks for that information. If we find the identity of the girl on the picture, we should be able to determine the link to Kelly and identify a possible location. If you don't mind, please wait here in my office and I'll come back to you shortly. Have you had time to drink or eat anything? Would you like me to arrange for a tea or a coffee for you?"

"Yes please, a tea would be great. That's kind, thank you. I'll wait here and see if anything comes to me in the meantime."

For the first time in the long hours since the nightmare started, Amanda felt a bit of hope coming back to her. If this was linked to Lisa, they might be able to find Kelly. She avoided dwelling on the fact that her young daughter might be held by the same person who had raped Lisa. She chose to focus on her hope that they might find Kelly alive. The deep fear that Kelly might be dead had lodged itself firmly inside her heart and showed no sign of leaving the nest. Suddenly, she was calm enough to attempt to connect with Kelly.

After a short while, the image of the abductor popped into her mind. He was tall, slim and wearing the same outfit she had seen on Lisa's abductor. He was wielding a knife and wearing the 'Scream mask' they had seen in the selfie earlier that day. The only other time, she had seen that particular mask was in her vision of Jamie's killer last September.

I've seen this before, it's almost the same vision as I got for Lisa. Except the mask is different. What does this mean? Oh, my God. That's it. That's what the message is about. It's about me finding out where Lisa was before the killer returned. I must tell DS Moon.

Rushing out of the office, she asked a passing officer to find DS Moon urgently for her. A few minutes later, the DS came out of the incident room to speak to her. He looked at her with a questioning look.

Words were tumbling out of Amanda's mouth.

"Kelly is with the man who raped Lisa. I've seen him. He is wearing a 'Scream mask' like in the selfie. I guess when I found Lisa, I disrupted his plans. That's why he's written spoilsport on the picture. Please we need to act fast. I am scared of what he'll do to Kelly. Hurry please. Did you find out anything?"

"The computer search confirmed Lisa Palmer was a rape victim from last October. The place where she was found was dark, she was found lying down, battered, on a dirty floor. The Polaroid picture fits in with the details we have. I have a hunch Kelly might be in the same place that Lisa was held. I have despatched officers to the arches right now. Please wait here and I'll get news to you as soon as I can. One of my colleagues will stay with you."

"I want to come with you. Please, I can't stay here and wait. I just can't!"

"Ms King, there's no certainty that Kelly is there. We'll let you know when we can."

"Please DS Moon, I have to be there. I have to find her with you. Please let me come. I can stay in the car, but I need to be there when you find her. And I know you will find her there. Please."

Her pleading got the better of the DS. "Wait here. I need to clear it and we'll go."

While waiting for Moon, Amanda paced the corridor ready to leave when he returned. Her heart was heavy and a dense feeling of foreboding was shrouding her. Within a few minutes, he was back and gave her the thumbs up. He escorted her past the reception area on the way to the car park.

At the front desk, a person was talking to the sergeant on duty. As they levelled with her, Amanda thought she heard the name Jamie Wilson. It made her pause for a brief moment, and glance at the female who was clearly upset, talking fast about several items in her bag. In mid-sentence, as if sensing she was being watched, the woman turned towards Amanda and their eyes met for a second. Prompted by Moon, Amanda walked on.

* * *

"Who is this woman? I wonder if she heard me. If she did, it's got nothing to do with her!"

Turning back to the duty sergeant, Karen Turner continued taking out a video tape and several items from her bag. She had asked to speak to the person in charge of the Jamie Wilson case. When asked why by the duty sergeant, she'd replied that she might have an idea who Jamie's killer was.

"That's my CCTV tape from last night. Several nights in a row recently, I had been hearing noises around the house. Coz my son Sam is rarely home, I got scared. I activated the cameras before going to bed last night. When I came home lunchtime today, I had an alert that the camera had detected movements. I saw Sam on the tape. It said he'd come in at 3.03 am today. I wouldn't have bothered about it, but when I looked at it closely again, I saw he was carrying a 'Scream mask'. Just like the one mentioned by the police when the boy Jamie was killed."

Karen had difficulty keeping her composure. She had been shocked by what she'd seen. Her mind had gone fuzzy, her heart numb, her whole body drained. She had watched the tape a few more times to make sure she wasn't mistaken. But there was no getting away from it. Sam had walked in early morning, carrying a 'Scream mask'. While Sam was at school, she had gone to search his room on a hunch. An unpleasant smell had filled her nostrils the minute she had stepped inside his bedroom. It wasn't weed this time. More like the sickly smell of vomit. She had gone around the room, sniffing here and there. The smell emanated from the wardrobe. Karen had looked inside but found nothing. She'd then pulled it out a bit and found several items crumpled up between the wardrobe and the wall.

"Maybe it's nothing, but as these things were hidden, I thought I'd better bring them to you. I found a strange mask, a tee-shirt smelling of vomit and this bloody underwear of Sam's. I saw him wearing it on Halloween night last year. That night, he threatened me with intense hatred in his eyes. I figured if he could attack his mother as he did, then I'm not 100% sure my son is incapable of killing another human being. Do you think the tape and his stuff will tell us whether Sam killed Jamie or not? Maybe I've got it all wrong."

Karen had agonised all lunchtime as to what to do. She had been shaken by the murder of the young boy last year and hoped that the killer would be found, if only for the sake of the parents. The plight of Jamie had touched her deeply. She loved Sam, but that incident last Halloween night had shown her a side of him she had been shaken by. She had asked herself many times if her son was a potential killer. The answer was yes every time. She was disgusted by her flesh and blood. Instead of going to her second job that afternoon, she had come to her local police station.

What mother turns her son in? What am I doing here? Maybe with what I brought the police today, they will put my mind to rest and prove Sam is innocent. Yes, that's it. This is gonna help prove his innocence. They have DNA tests now, they can prove it one way or another.

The duty sergeant interrupted her thoughts.

"Sit down please, Ma'am. I'll get an officer to come and talk to you. Can I take your name first?"

[22]

Two police cars arrived at the railway arch where Lisa Palmer had been held. Three officers from the investigation team went in. It was dark. At first, it was impossible to see anything. Using big torches, they advanced into the cavernous, cold space. The silence around them was eerie. Their steps echoed. They walked slowly towards the centre of the disused workshop. One officer, Mark White, heard a squelching sound as he moved forward. Shining his torch on the floor, he saw a puddle of red fluid spread out under his right foot. He gasped.

"Over here sergeant."

The other two followed the light from his torch and saw a pool of blood. They shined the luminous beam further into the darkness. What they saw made their stomach turn. The newest recruit of the three rushed outside, holding his hand in front of his mouth, retching noises reverberating in the darkness.

The more-seasoned officer, Rob Davies, looked at the unwelcome sight with sadness in their hearts. A young girl was lying on the floor, covered in blood. It looked as if she had been stabbed multiple times.

"Mark, get the DS. That must be Kelly."

While his colleague dashed out, Davies approached the young victim. It looked like she had bled to death from the stab wounds. No matter how many bodies he had seen in his career, when it came to a child, it always got to him. Davies made a sign of the cross, praying for the soul of the child to be at peace.

Moon came in, taking in the tragic sight inside. As he was approaching closer to Kelly's body, he heard a commotion outside by the door. He recognised Amanda's voice. She was hysterical, and the officer by the door struggled to hold her back.

"Kelly? Kelly? Let me see her. She's inside, I know she is. I need to see my child, please. Let me go!"

Hearing Amanda, Moon rushed to the doorway to prevent her from entering and seeing Kelly. The look on his face told Amanda all she needed to know.

"Ms King, I'm so sorry."

Moon had to hold Amanda firmly back as she

wrestled with him to get to her daughter. Tears were streaming down her face.

"Please don't go in, you can't see Kelly like that. We have to get a forensic team here now. Let me get an officer to take you home. There is nothing you can do here. Please Ms King, let the police and the coroner deal with Kelly. You'll see her later. "

Being a father himself, Moon understood Amanda's desperate need to see and hold her child one last time. But he couldn't allow her to touch the body. It was part of the crime scene. He signalled to his colleague to take Amanda away from the door. White propped up a sobbing Amanda, walking her towards a waiting police car. The sudden, primal sound which came from the bottom of her being, was not a sound Amanda recognised. No officer within earshot of the distraught mother, had ever heard such depth of despair, pain and sorrow held in one howl. Walking like a zombie, between sobs Amanda kept repeating: "We're too late. Kelly's gone."

Moon called Styles to inform him of the tragic outcome. He added that Amanda would be driven home shortly to be with to her husband and her mother. Moon's job was nearly done at the scene, and he needed to return to Croydon Police Station. Right now, he wanted Amanda away from here. The coroner was awaiting the go-ahead from the SOCO to remove the body as soon as the forensics' job was done, and he wanted to spare Amanda this distressing sight. Obviously, the child had to be formally identified as Kelly, so both parents would see her in the mortuary. Various forensic tests would be carried out, before the body was released for burial. Moon's task right now was to find as many clues as possible to identify the killer. It was tragic, and he had hoped for a different outcome. The abduction was now classified as a homicide. Moon swore to make it his mission to find the person responsible.

Making his way out of the archway, Moon saw Amanda get into the police car, relieved she was leaving the scene. Lost in his thoughts he hadn't paid attention to the insistent ringing of his mobile phone. He recognised the number for Croydon Police Station. He answered abruptly.

"DS Moon. "

"Sir, it's Maria Garcia, at the front counter. Sorry to disturb you. A woman called Karen Turner is talking to one of the Detective Constables. She thinks her teenage son might have killed Jamie Wilson as he has a 'Scream mask'. Matt, in the incident room, told me earlier that the abductor of the young child you're looking for had a 'Scream mask'. I thought it best to let you know. Any news on the child, Sir?

"Yes. We found her body. Multiple stab wounds. I'm on my way back. Make sure Ms Turner stays at the station until I can talk to her. I'll be there shortly. And, Maria, thanks for letting me know."

* * *

Styles greeted Amanda when she arrived back home, and witnessed the emotional reunion of the bereaved parents and grandmother. He had already informed Nathan and Reine that Kelly had been found dead from multiple stab wounds. To say that this information had elicited a pained reaction from both was an understatement. Usually, he loved his job, but on days like today, it stank to be part of such tragedy, to witness the evil acts that deranged human beings are capable of. It upset him to see decent people filled with such sorrow, and to hear the agonising exchange between the three of them.

The minute she walked into the flat, Amanda threw herself into Nathan's arms and brought her mother into a tight embrace. They hung onto one another, in desperation, to cope with the trauma of what had just happened. The circle they formed was helping them stay up. Their world had crumbled, and the three of them were about to collapse too. Amidst her tears, in panic mode, struggling to breathe, Amanda could only repeat the same words.

"Kelly's gone. Our girl's gone. He's killed her. I couldn't stop him."

With each word she uttered, her sobs doubled in intensity. She was remembering Kelly's fate over and over. She was on the verge of collapsing despite being held by Nathan.

"Shush, you did what you could, Amanda. The cops didn't get to her in time. I want to get my hands on the bastard for what he did to our baby girl. I want to go out there, find him and fucking kill him. My beautiful girl, my poor, poor girl."

The wail Nathan emitted was gut-wrenching for those around him. He tightened his grip on Amanda, his voice distorted by anguish and rage.

Reine too was holding on to Amanda, tears falling slowly and steadily. She was in shock, still processing what she was hearing, but had not yet reached the hysterical stage that Amanda was in. She heard Amanda ask her a question she had asked herself many times since Styles had given her the terrible news:

"Mum, why didn't we find her before it was too late? We saw where she was, why didn't we know she was in such danger? How come we couldn't help her?"

"Darling, I don't know for sure, but sometimes spirits of people who love us very much, want to spare us from seeing the bad thing happening to them. Maybe Kelly wanted to spare you an awful, distressing vision of what she endured."

In trying to justify their failure to Amanda, Reine's composure finally crumbled and she felt an intense grief envelop her.

* * *

On his return to the station, Moon found which Detective Constable was dealing with Karen Turner. His colleague, DC Agbo, was currently taking a statement from the woman. He had been in the process of finishing off the interview when he had been told DS Moon wanted to speak to him and Ms Turner. Agbo brought him up to speed with what he had learned so far.

"In her statement, Ms Turner has named her son, Sam Turner, 16 years old, as the potential killer of Jamie Wilson. He was caught on her CCTV camera coming home in the early hours of this morning, carrying a 'Scream mask'. She remembered hearing that Jamie's suspected killer had worn one and that, at the time, the public had been warned to be vigilant. That's why it rang alarm bells with her."

As a result of her statement, Agbo had placed in evidence bags the various items Ms Tuner had brought in that belonged to her son. There was a tee-shirt sporting traces of vomit and a terrible smell. She had pointed out that this item may or may not be related to an illegal activity. She had handed over a 'Smiley mask' and a pair of men's underwear with blood on them, stating they had all been hidden behind Sam's wardrobe. She had thought that by bringing in the tape and the items, it would be possible with DNA to know for sure if Sam had committed a murder or not. All the evidence would be sent to forensics to extract fingerprints and any DNA presence. She was hoping that it would eliminate Sam as a suspect.

After talking briefly to Agbo outside the interview room, both men entered and sat opposite Karen. She looked up at them with apprehension. Moon smiled at her, hoping to put her at ease.

"For the benefit of the tape, it is now 4.20 pm on June 29th 2017 and Detective Sergeant Moon has joined Detective Constable Agbo to carry on the interview of Ms Karen Turner.

Ms Turner, I have briefed DS Moon on the statement you have made. He has a few questions to ask you before you leave the station. Is that okay?"

Karen nodded in the direction of Moon.

"Thank you, Ms Turner. I understand from your statement that you believe your son, Sam, may have committed a murder and more specifically Jamie Wilson's murder. The fact that you saw CCTV footage from your home camera which shows Sam carrying a 'Scream mask' is the reason you are suspicious. However, it's quite an assumption. What you saw on last night's tape, is important and you did right to bring it to us. Only forensics will tell us if he is responsible for Jamie's murder. But I need to ask you, Ms Turner, has Sam displayed any behaviour in the past. or more recently, which would lead you to believe he is capable of an act of murder?"

"Well, Sam's always been difficult. He's been a challenging kid from a toddler. He has ADHD. You must understand, I had to raise him alone coz his father wasn't around much when Sam was growing up. Then later he gave him bad habits like getting him to smoke cannabis. I argued with Sam and his father all the time about the smoking. I told Sam to stop but he turned against me. It doesn't make him a killer, I know. But last Halloween night he came home late, extremely angry. He was changing his clothes when I went into his room. I noticed he was wearing a pair of briefs which were covered with blood. I thought he'd started self-harming again like he used to. I said nothing. But a few minutes after that, we got into an argument. I lost my rag, told him to piss off to his father's. I called him an evil child. I don't know why. I'm not proud of it. It just escaped me. Probably coz he often scares me. He is disrespectful. Maybe he was pissed off I had seen him in his underwear. Anyway, as he threatened me physically, I backed off on the landing. I was at the top of the stairs and he was lunging towards me. He was in such a rage, that I thought he was going to push me down the stairs. "

"Can you confirm the exact date and approximate time when this incident took place, Ms Turner?" Agbo butted in.

"As I said, it was Halloween last year, 2016. He'd gone out with his mates and I warned him not to get home late as he had school the next day. He showed up after 9 o'clock. Went straight to his room, in a foul mood. Then we had that argument, and he left to stay at his dad's."

"Anything else which makes you believe Sam is capable of having carried out Jamie's murder?"

"No. Well, maybe. I'm not sure. His father has let him watch horror films since he was a kid. When he is at his father's, Sam spends his time watching unsuitable films, playing creepy video games or smoking weed. When he is at school, he gets in trouble too."

The description of the boy's character given by his mother was ringing alarm bells in Moon's mind. Maybe he was putting two and two together and making five, but there were quite a few links which were beyond coincidence. Kelly's bear had been left in the guesthouse where Jamie was killed. Coincidence? How about the mention of the Spiderman bag? If Sam had indeed killed Jamie, he would have known about those two things. But the 'Smiley mask' found behind his wardrobe had been used by Lisa's rapist. What was Sam's connection to Lisa? Was it again a coincidence that the boy had come back with blood on his underwear on Halloween night? And he had been in an aggressive mood, enough to threaten his mother and scare her witless. He was certain there was a strong link between Jamie's killer, Lisa's rapist and Kelly's killer. He knew one link was Amanda King who had worked on two cases and Kelly was her daughter. DNA evidence was needed to prove the exact nature of Sam's involvement in the three incidents. If he was Kelly's killer, they had to get to him fast.

"Ms Turner, where is Sam now? We need to talk to him."

"He should be finishing school for the day. They have end-of-year exams this week. He goes to St Joseph's in Peckham Rye."

"We need to contact the school and find Sam urgently. DC Agbo please pause the interview for now and contact the school. We'll take a break now, Ms Turner. Can I get you a glass of water or a hot drink?"

Karen shook her head.

"No thanks. I want to get on with this and go home to Sam."

"Alright. Interview suspended at 4.30 pm. DC Agbo has left the room and DS Moon remaining with Ms Turner."

What Moon had learnt from Agbo and from interviewing Karen Turner, was giving him hope. He was convinced that he might be able to find Kelly's killer earlier than he had thought. He trusted his instinct and the revelations he'd just heard were huge, he could not ignore them.

* * *

"St Joseph's School Secretary. Can I help you?"

"Good afternoon. My name is DC Agbo from Croydon Police Station. We are looking for one of your pupils, Sam Turner? Can you please check if he is at school now?"

"I can tell you straight away, Sam Turner is not here. He left school before lunch and has not returned. Since lunchtime, I've been ringing his mother but there's no answer on the home number. We tried her work number, but she did not show up to work today. No joy with Mr Warnham, his father, either. Is it to do with Aimee Palmer?"

[23]

Sam's epic journey had come to an end. He was running on adrenaline from the buzz of the treasure hunt and getting his revenge. By now Kelly's body would have been found.

I wished I'd seen the medium's face. I bet she got the message by now. Let see how long it takes them to work it all out. Never thought I had it in me. Wow! I'm smarter and stronger than I imagined. But I'm tired now.

He had changed his mind about going to Karen's. Instead, he rode his bike to Ben's flat and arrived around 5.30 pm. He returned the bike to the cellar just as he had found it. The trailer had been disposed of the previous night, in an overgrown grassed area, on his way back to his mother's. The mask, the knife, the camera and his blood-stained clothes were hidden in his bag, at the back of the cellar.

Right, that takes care of everything. Job well done, man. Hell, you need a joint. Badly. Come on, you have to calm down. You're too excited. Chill, you're here now. Go play Slender Man. See how lame that is now you've done the real thing.

The flat was empty, and Sam went straight to the stash of weed in his dad's safe place. He took a good helping of it, settled in front of his computer and rolled himself a joint. He smoked it with delight, inhaling each puff deeply, savouring its strong, pungent taste. His overexcited mind was beginning to mellow under the influence of cannabis. Slender man was grinning back at him on the screen. He heard the front door slam. Ben walked straight into the front room, talking on his mobile and ignoring Sam in his room.

A short while later a loud knock on the front door disrupted Sam's game.

"Dad, are you gonna get it? Dad?"

Through the partly-open door of this bedroom, Sam caught a glimpse of Ben making his way to the front door. He was coming down from the adrenaline high he had been on the last couple of days. Up until now, there had been no place in his heart or mind for scruples, fear or remorse. Now he was crashing back to earth and was shivering from head to toe. The reality of what he had done and of his situation hit him. If the cops were at the door, his life was over. It was a sobering thought. But would they come for him so soon? His mind was full of fog as if his brain was wrapped in cotton wool, filling up the entire space in his skull. He was unable to think, talk or move. His body had gone dead and heavy.

Wow, that's quite strong shit my dad's got. Maybe I used a bit too much or it's stronger than usual.

From a remote place in this brain, he heard the front door being opened, his dad raising his voice and unknown voices answering back. He was unable to make out anything that was being said.

A man in a suit, waving a police badge, came into his room. The man stood in front of him, talking to him. Sam knew the man was talking, his lips were moving, but his brain did not register the words. He looked at the big man and the police officer who'd appeared behind him. They beckoned for him to follow them out.

Sweet! It's over. They've found the body. She knows now why I retaliated and we're even.

Sam, flanked by both police officers was escorted, with his father, to a police car waiting outside the block of flats. The boy heard the sounds of an angry voice. He turned towards Ben sitting next to him. He was aware Ben was talking angrily to him but his brain was still frozen in this faraway place where nothing made sense. At this moment, only one question pierced through the fog in Sam's brain.

What's gonna happen to me?

* * *

After his arrest and having given a statement, Sam was sent to juvenile detention. There he waited to hear if he would appear in front of a youth court as he was a minor or the Crown Court. It would depend on the severity of the "grave crimes" he had committed.

Moon had to wait to receive all the evidence for the investigation to progress and determine how many cases Sam Turner was involved in. His mother had been concerned he had killed Jamie Wilson. Unknowingly, Karen had given the police vital evidence about Sam's involvement in Lisa's rape and Kelly's murder.

Karen Turner almost had a breakdown when Moon informed her of the possible three crimes her son had committed. He had seen distraught parents in his many years in the job, but the reaction of this particular mother would stay with him for a long time. His heart went out to her. A mother handing her son on a plate to the police was a tough cross to bear for the rest of her life.

When the forensic results finally came back, DNA recovered on the 'Scream mask' proved to be from Sam. But a strand of hair recovered on the mask did not match anyone on the DNA database. When asked if he knew who the unknown person might be, Sam shrugged his shoulders and said he had no idea. Moon did not believe him but it didn't really matter at this stage. There was more than enough evidence to charge Sam with Jamie Wilson's murder.

Lisa's DNA had been found alongside Sam's, on the bloody underwear. The 'Smiley mask' had revealed a tiny spec of blood, later found to belong to Lisa Palmer. Together with the semen sample, this provided enough evidence to charge Sam with her rape. When Sam's phone was examined by the police, they had discovered pictures of Lisa taken during and after her ordeal.

From the soiled clothing Karen Turner had brought in, forensics were able to determine that the vomit on Sam's top came from Kelly. The knife and other items had since been recovered when officers raided the cellar. On the strength of the overwhelming evidence, Sam had been charged with Kelly Stark's abduction and murder.

Moon had been coordinating the prosecution case, even though it involved different police stations. With two charges of murder and one of rape, it was not possible to hold the trial in a youth court. The crimes were deemed serious offences and the Crown Prosecution Services (CPS) decided to prosecute Sam Turner in the Crown Court. He was a minor, but he was at the age of criminal responsibility. The judge dealt with Sam under the dangerous offender provisions and had given him a life custodial sentence. He had been appalled that a young man had carried out such violent acts on such young victims. Not only that, but the fact that Sam has staged a wild goose chase for the police and for the parents of the child, knowing that he had already killed her, showed psychopathic tendencies. Therefore, the interest of the public would be best served with Sam locked up for the rest of his life. The CPS had been elated with the judge's decision. The penal system would decide whether to send Sam to a secure Young Offender Institution or to incarcerate him in an adult prison despite being a minor. At the trial, a social worker had described Sam's past disruptive and inappropriate behaviour while at school. A psychiatrist had testified that Sam knew right from wrong and was deemed responsible for his actions. The influence of drugs from a young age, poor parenting, the diagnosis of ADHD, and a lack of a strong role model from the beginning had been contributing factors to his committing the crimes.

Both Karen and Ben had attended the trial and kept a low profile in the public gallery. On the CPS side, Amanda, Nathan and Reine sat together. The parents of Jamie Wilson, and of Lisa Palmer, attended the trial too. All of them were devastated when hearing the details of each crime, somehow reliving their own nightmare. But when the coroner announced that the time of Kelly's death was around 11 am on 29th June 2017, as Kelly had been killed at the start of the treasure hunt, everyone wondered why give her parents the false hope of finding her alive. To many of the people in the gallery, this revealed an even more shocking evil streak in the accused.

The press were aware of the three crimes Sam had been charged with. Before the trial started, Moon had been shocked at the way the media treated Amanda King. Instead of concentrating on Sam and the deeds he had committed, the newspapers made jokes out of the situation with headlines like "Psychic's daughter murdered; she did not see it coming!" Many times, he questioned what made reporters tick. This was a distressing time for Kelly's family and friends without having to contend with poor taste jokes.

Moon knew that for Amanda, not getting to Kelly on time, was an open wound likely to fester for many years. He suspected that this poor mother would live with that pain every waking second, minute and hour of the day, even of the night, from now on. He was pleased when the media finally moved on to another story.

***

Throughout the trial, Ben had been stunned to hear the details of the attacks Sam had carried out. Despite the gruesome details of the crimes his son had committed, it seemed that Ben was more upset by being the owner of the bike used by Sam to facilitate the transport of his victim than by the actual crime. Ben was also upset that the bag containing all the items relating to Kelly's killing had been found in his cellar. Even with the poor opinion Ben had of his 16 year-old son, he had never imagined Sam capable of killing and raping. As Ben lived in a world filled with drugs and crime, he had a little shred of admiration for his kid who had the guts to do a deed of that magnitude. Hearing the experts talk about Sam's upbringing made him question if he had been a bad father. He had done his best for his boy. In his head, he kept remembering Karen criticising his poor parenting over the years.

KAREN - 2018

EPILOGUE

After many attempts to schedule a visit, Karen managed to get a pass to see Sam in HM Prison Feltham. He was serving his time in the Young Offenders Institution, housed there. It would be her first visit with him since Sam had been convicted of the murders.

Having travelled by underground and train to reach Feltham, Karen arrived rather flustered for her visit. She was a bit early and was asked to wait until her allocated time. She was nervous. She had rehearsed many things to say to Sam. Every time she thought of him, the river of tears threatened to burst its bank.

Right now, she focussed on her surroundings, hoping to bring her emotions in check before seeing Sam. Despite the low brick building being less foreboding than a traditional prison, there was still an air of gloominess and hopelessness about it. Visitors waited huddled on uncomfortable chairs. The faces of family members visiting their loved ones had the same expression of desperation and puzzlement. How did they find themselves in this waiting room? A guard was standing by the door, ushering the visitors into the visiting room for their given appointment.

At 2 pm, Karen was shown to a small room with booths. There was only one chair on either side and a tall glass screen ran the length of the booths, separating the visitors from the prisoners. She had expected to sit opposite Sam like she had seen in films, so this set-up was disappointing. She saw Sam, on the other side of the screen, further along, and made her way to the fourth booth. She sat down opposite him. He was keeping his head down, not willing to look at her. She picked up the phone hanging on her right and knocked on the glass screen, nudging Sam to do the same.

"Hello, Sam."

"Hi, Mum."

The sadness in his voice and his downcast demeanour caught her by surprise. She had been so used to his arrogance and defiance, that she had forgotten how it was to speak to Sam in a normal, non-confrontational way. Her heart ached for him.

"How are you doing, son?"

"What d'you think?" The defiance was back.

"Why did you do it, Sam? How could you kill the two little kids, Jamie and Kelly, in such a savage way? Why rape the other young girl? Why Sam? What possessed you?"

She had not meant to blurt out all of this the minute she saw him, but she had tormented herself with these questions since Sam had been arrested. She was hoping that visiting him might finally bring her the answers she needed.

"Why do you care about the reasons why? You're like the cops, the lawyers, the shrinks, the guards. WHY? That's all everyone wants to know. It's a bit late to worry about why I did what I did. It's done! Tell me, Mum, why did you have me? Why did you hate me? Why was I never good enough for you? Answer me those WHYs and maybe I'll answer yours."

Karen had not expected that sort of reaction from Sam. After what the shrink had said at the trial, she had wondered why she had gone from being Sam's mother to being the mother of a child killer. She wasn't sure what she had done wrong apart from working too hard since he was born. Karen had told

Ben a few days ago that it was mostly his fault. She was hoping Sam would explain to her why he had committed these shocking crimes.

"Sam, I never hated you. But I struggled coz you were a difficult kid. A kid with a bad attitude. We couldn't talk to each other and you were often rude to me. I'm sorry you felt unloved. I'm sorry I had no time for you growing up. I did my best, bringing you up alone most of the time."

"There we go again. It's easy to always blame Dad but take a good look at yourself! You were never there. I got no advice from you, no love, nothing… Anyway, I've had enough of this conversation. Don't bother coming back. Guard, I'm done."

"Sam, wait. Please just tell me one thing. Why did you do it?

"You wanna know why I did it, Mum? Because I am fucking clever and because I could!

Karen remained on the seat, stunned by Sam's retort. After a few minutes, the guard asked her to leave. She walked out of the prison, dazed, knowing in her heart that she would never see her son again.

***

Going back to his cell, Sam found an envelope on his bed. By now, he knew several guards were partial to bribery. A few of them delivered letters to prisoners for the right price, and without scrutinising them too closely. He thought it might be one of those, but who from?

In the envelope, he retrieved a roll-up cigarette and a piece of paper. Sam unfolded it and read "Thanks for taking the rap for Jamie. Enjoy the joint. J."

ACKNOWLEDGEMENTS

Dear Reader,

Thank you for choosing my book and I hope you enjoyed the story.

Your feedback is welcome, so feel free to leave a review on my Facebook page, Andrée Roby@RegineDem, on Amazon, or on Goodreads. Thank you.

"Double Vision" is available on Amazon, as well as my "A to Z of original poems, flash fiction and short stories".

Until the next book, all the best.

Andrée x

Printed in Poland
by Amazon Fulfillment
Poland Sp. z o.o., Wrocław